TRIP TRAP

TRIP TRAP
Farrukh Dhondy

LONDON
VICTOR GOLLANCZ LTD
1984

© Farrukh Dhondy 1982

First published October 1982
Second impression April 1984

British Library Cataloguing in Publication Data
Dhondy, Farrukh
  Trip Trap.
  I. Title
  823'[F]

ISBN 0-575-03193-X

Photoset in Great Britain by
Rowland Phototypesetting Ltd, Bury St Edmunds, Suffolk
and printed by St Edmundsbury Press
Bury St Edmunds, Suffolk

Contents

Herald

Herald

"In India they'll be having Dassera now," my dad says, just to pass the time like.

"What's that?" Kenny goes. He likes listening to my dad's stories about his village and that.

"It is one festival for machines."

"Don't get it."

"You dress up the machines with garland and flowers and everything. Make the god of machines happy. Even pets. I used to have one bicycle in the house and at Dassera we dressed it up."

"Dressed the bloomin' bicycle?" Kenny goes. "That's bloody loopy. On our puppy's birthday my sister dressed the mong up in dad's T shirt. Bleeder crapped in it.'

"If you look after tools, they will look after you," my dad says. I know he's about to start, so I says I want to go round to the games section again.

"Stylish," Kenny goes. It's his word.

That was the first night we went up to the biggest industrial exhibition in London. There's cars, machines, hoovers that walk round on their own, all sorts of gear and the computers and the games. We got in for nothing, 'cause my dad had a job there as a security guard. Three nights we went there and Kenny and I stuck in the games section. My dad was a bit nervous like because he didn't want the other guards to think he was taking liberties.

My dad thought that since Kenny and I was always messing around with chemistry sets and electronic kits and that, we'd like to check out all the gear at the exhibition. It was holidays so my mum and Kenny's mum didn't say nothing—well they didn't say much.

My dad had to sit in this cabin with white plastic walls. It had a smart fire alarm panel, a sort of map of the whole place and it could tell you the temperature in any part of the exhibition and if there was a fire like it would flash and the automatic control would come on and put the fire out. Dad was told that he didn't have to do nothing, it would see to itself. He just had to press buttons to set off the alarm and call the fire engines in case something didn't work right.

The first night we just fiddled with the position finders. They were the best thing there and everyone who came to see the exhibition could borrow one. Like a wrist watch, it had a small TV screen which would tell you where you were when you pressed a button and a picture of the nearest exit would flash on your wrist. Neat. But, nah, that wasn't the best thing. There was this computer in the games section called Herald. It was made to tell stories. It starts when you stand in front of it and a weird voice comes out, soft, like someone trying to hypnotise you. It introduces itself to you, 'cause it knows you're there and then you can introduce yourself back and it gets to know you.

Shall I tell you one of my stories? It's about a boy called Dipak. He came to this great exhibition. No? You don't want that one? Oliver Twist? A Christmas Carol? Romeo and Juliet. Wimpy stories? Slackness. Explain that word please.

It was great. It would rearrange words like they ought to be. First time I couldn't think of nothing, so I said, "All right, LAMB, LITTLE, HAD, MARY, A. That's It." So I says to it, pressing the rearrange button, "Straighten that out, headbanger."

And the computer goes: "That's it. Mary had an all right little lamb."

"Not an all right lamb, you div," I says.

So he goes, "Mary didn't have an all right little lamb."

Stroppy kid.

I called Kenny. He was on this Deadly Aquarium machine what you stood in like a tunnel and the sharks and monsters came at you out of the seaweed and from behind the rocks. They looked like real ones and you had buttons to shoot them down and it looked like actual blood come out of them when you harpooned the monsters. He likes stuff like that, Kenny. He got sixty quid last Christmas from his uncles and big brothers and on my life he spent every last penny on the blinkin' Space Invaders machines.

"Come here," I goes. "If you let it watch you it will tell you all sorts of thing about what it sees."

Kenny has jeans and a red and yellow scarf. He smiles
and his beautiful white teeth flash in an endearing
expression . . .

"I think it fancies you," I goes.

"Get away," he goes and wants to get back to the Deadlies but I'd already taught Herald some slackness so I switch on the recent memory and Herald starts up in this soupy voice: "Kenny is a flash c---"

"Takes one to know one," Kenny goes. "Wally machine. You're a flash c---"

What you should do is tell it a whole story or just give it jumbled up things and it would sort them into a kind of story. I messed about with it all night. The things what the people what made it had fed into it were boring. All history stories and that.

11

Trip Trap

This is the story of the great fire that overtook the first exhibition of industry in London in the eighteenth century. Many stories were told about that fire. Some people believed that god was angry because the exhibition was a boast. Human beings were showing off . . ."

It could natter on. We fetched my dad and got him to tell Herald one of his stories. We had a job getting him out of the cabin and up to the games section 'cause he was scared that they'd give him the sack if he left the fire panel thing. But in the end he came and he thought it was smart too. When we played it back it started pretending it was my dad talking.

It was in my village in India in my father's time. There was flood after the rains came and the water covered all the fields and houses. Just like the water spreads, the rumours used to spread. When I was a boy there was a superstition in the village that a creature called the crow woman was going about at night. Stupid people thought that the crow woman had the body of a crow and the head of a woman with long black hair and frightening black teeth. It would come at night and call out to a person in a voice which they would recognise. It would shout 'help' or 'emergency' and you would think it was your friend or your brother and if you answered or went outside it would get you.

"You want to rub that story out," Kenny says. "This place is weird enough without the Herald johnny coming with ghost stories."

"You can't," I says, "Herald learns as he goes. It can't forget."

"Tomorrow when the public come in, some geezer's going to get a shock if it repeats your dad's stories. They'll know we've been getting at the machines."

"I think it changes the stories. Just learns new words off of us."

So my dad says he wants to get back to the cabin and he doesn't know how to operate the position finder gizmo, so Kenny says he'll show him and I go off to find the loo on my TV dial. That's on the second night.

One person can know only so many stories. Everything that happens can be retold. With one keyboard you make an endless number of tunes. There are only two hundred and eighty seven basic plots. The Queen dies, then the king dies. Those are facts. The king dies and the Queen dies of heartache, that's a story. Programme X2115938K.

"So what happens if you just read it the whole dictionary. If it's so smart, it can tell all the stories, all the books ever wrote."

"Yeah, we'll try it tomorrow."

"You'll do writers out of a job."

"That's good. *I* wouldn't mind a machine doing my work for me."

"You know the tune that's on top of the charts. I heard this geezer on telly who said a computer wrote it and he's got thousands of other top tunes out of it."

The lights in this place are automatic. They come on in front of you as you walk and switch off once you pass. When I come out of the bog now, this was on the third day, right, I get this kind of sweetish smell like you get off some shirts when the iron's too hot. And when I got on to the escalator to the upper level it wasn't working. I looked at my position reckoner and the red dot was leading me up to the household section. The lights were coming on all right, and it looked kind of misty on top. When I got up, my eyes began stinging and I felt like my breathing was getting rough. It was smoke in the corner and suddenly like in clouds. So I turned and ran down the escalator. There was smoke coming down it too, like a stream following me. I thought about what dad had said about the automatic fire business and I ran to the other escalator. It was no use shouting, though, 'cause the other security guards wouldn't have heard me as dad said they'd be up the office playing cards. I was frightened, I'll give you that. I was tapping the position reckoner to see which way out, but the smoke was getting thick down in the basement level now. Then there was a sound like a giant walking on twigs and a kind of whistling.

When he found himself in a small clearing in the basement he took a deep breath of fresh air. He could see the wax dummies in the basement operating machines by the green and red lights of the panels they were working. Dad and Kenny must still be in the games section. Inside that Deadly Aquarium you wouldn't know of any danger outside. Now the smoke was as thick as a quilt. The lights of the panels began to look hazy, like traffic signals in a fog. He looked up the escalator and he thought the smoke seemed to have cleared. It must be the automatic fire control.

The panic in him drained away and he began thinking clearly. Like the clear head you get after the first flash of red in a fight. You know what you have to do. At the top of the escalator there was a lit arch. The smoke had cleared and Dipak went through the arch into a passage between plastic walls, made out of bits which were locked together like a puzzle. He thought he knew where he was. There was a room at the end of the passage. He rushed towards it. Now he was sure that he hadn't been there before, he was thinking of the same sort of passage on another level.

He entered the room. It was like no other in the exhibition. It was just ordinary with a pool table and a fruit machine and a kitchen unit with a kettle and an urn on top and coffee cups on the three wooden tables. There were people there. Six of them. It must be the Security Guards' rest room. They were weird people.

"There's a fire. The place is on fire," Dipak said. "Mr Patel. There's a fire."

"Don't panic, child, there's no fire. This place is fully automated, proof against all disasters." This was an old lady in a boiler suit.

"There's human error, it might be some bloody short circuit—these fumblers . . ." A young man with a punk hair cut and green streaks in his hair said, but he was interrupted by a youngish lady.

"What kind of work do you do, boy?"

"I'm at school," Dipak said.

"Keeps you out of mischief," the young woman said.

"The fire . . ." Dipak began.

"Explain to the boy," the old lady said.

No one volunteered to explain so the old woman started off herself.

"Shall we let him hang about? He could probably give us some good advice. Look, boy . . ."

"You're too soft on humans," the young lady said to the old one. "Tell him to clear off."

"I'm sorry, I didn't . . ." Dipak said.

"No, relax," the big man said. "Industria might have something there. If we can't settle it amongst ourselves, the boy could give us some indication, some hints."

"What hints?" Dipak asked.

"We don't normally ask advice from mere human beings," the old lady said, "but let me introduce you."

She walked up to Dipak and with one hand gently placed on his shoulder she went round the room.

"That's Telos, Nukita, Mobo, Calcus, Balencia and I'm Industria. Some of the others couldn't come. Telos, Nukita and Calcus, as you can see, are young ones, inexperienced, I would say . . ."

"Now hang about," Telos said.

"Let her finish, for god's sake, you are always interrupting," said Mobo, the middle-aged fat man.

"I was saying, boy," the old lady said, "we are having a conference."

"Who are you? You're not the guards?" Dipak asked.

"It should become obvious," the old lady said. "I'm Industria, I've lived for thousands of years. I'm a goddess."

"Get away," Dipak said.

"I can't," the old lady said, "not till we've resolved this question. You see Telos and Calcus are fed up with you lot. Telos is the god of things seen and things unseen at a distance. Calcus is the god of all logic. Calcus has this plan to do away with all human beings. He says they're not much use to us any more."

"That's not what I said," Calcus interrupted, "but if you take all things to their logical end, we don't need thinking animals any more. The machines can do it."

"We need working hands," Industria said.

"Not even those, soon," said the lady called Balencia. "If you'd just get on with what you have to do, we can soon have machines making machines. No nonsense, no people to go on strike, make mistakes, demand training, spoil everything with their filth."

"Can't you see it?" Telos said. "A million television sets with life as it should be going on and no one to watch and think and misunderstand. Twenty four hours a day, every day of the year, everywhere."

"You see, they want to get rid of you," Industria said with a sigh. "I don't think we're ready for that yet."

"I'm ready," Nukita said. "Just give me the word."

"We're doing a good job of killing them off slowly. Do you know how many people died in car and rail and plane accidents last year?"

"We don't want to know. I don't like all this relish of death. It's all right on the screen, but in real life . . . it's unnecessary," Telos said.

"There's no relish left in it mate," Mobo said. "When the Titanic sank, slowly, people panicking, jumping overboard. Oh dear yes, those were the days."

"You're distracting the boy," Industria said. "The question we want to ask you, boy, is do you want to do any work when you . . . well when you finish school and training or whatever. What do the rest of you think, your generation?"

"Kenny don't want to do no work," Dipak said. "He'd be quite happy watching telly and playing space invaders and new games and that."

"You see?" Telos said. "They've become unnecessary. Balencia will be quite happy if there are vegetables and plants and trees and non-interfering animals around. We wipe out, Nukita wipes out the human race and we pretend it hasn't happened by keeping the telly sets on. If we get lonely for human beings, we watch old films."

"There'll be no one to drive around and . . ." Mobo started.

"That's not much to lose," Telos interrupted. "You can get together and make rockets which fly on their own, plant computers and machines all over the universe, on other planets, on other stars. These humans are locked in by time. They don't think big. Time doesn't matter to us, we can take millions of years to populate the other planets."

"That's the most convincing argument I've heard this evening," Industria said, "but I don't think we can start immediately. We have to get human beings to set it all up for us and then, bang, we can get rid of them."

"How much time do you need?" Balencia asked.

"We're more than halfway there," Industria replied. "Soon everything will be automatic and then people will just become a nuisance to each other and to us. Say ten years?"

"Too long. Much too long," Nukita said. She was thoughtful. "I'll wait two or three years. You'll just have to get them to work faster at it."

"That's difficult," said Calcus. "They might catch on to what we're up to and act up. After all, so far they've created the machines and the machines have created us. If they get wind of the master plan, they can screw it up. If they smash all the nuclear weapons, for instance, just as an example, mind you, no offence intended, Nukita would cease to exist."

"Well they won't get wind of the plan. They're not that smart. The only way is if the boy goes out and tells them."

And the company turned to Dipak, but he was gone.

He looked back when he'd got down the escalator. He could hear footsteps behind him. His heart was thumping and he could feel it in his throat.

"Dippy," he heard Kenny's voice.

"Down here," Dipak shouted.

The smoke was unbearable. He had to shut his eyes which stung worse than soap getting in them. He felt for the walls and walked towards Kenny's voice.

He felt he was about to faint because he was holding his breath and his lungs were bursting. He didn't know if he actually fainted, but he knew that he felt strong arms lifting him up. They've got hold of me, he thought, I'll be the first to go.

"I've got him," he heard a voice shout. He thought it was Telos's voice.

Outside, Dipak opened his stinging eyes. Kenny's face and the face of two firemen were bent over him and the world spun round like he'd just come off a whirligig. Only at the hospital, when they were being tipped into their beds, did Dipak notice that his arms and legs were burnt and his clothes were torn.

"My dad . . ."

"Not a scratch. He's all right," the doctor said. "Hold still."

That evening the television cameras and the reporters crowded into the ward and talked to Kenny and Dipak. The doctor asked Dipak and Kenny first and let them in two at a time. One of the reporters had punk hair and a green streak in it and the lady with him reminded Dipak of someone. She was an oldish lady with a wise face.

"It's a miracle how you boys got out alive," she said. "Will you answer one or two questions?"

"What's happened to the games section?" Kenny asked.

"The whole exhibition was gutted," the lady replied.

"The Deadly Aquarium?" Kenny asked.

"It's was just plastic. Finished. Funnily enough the only thing the fire didn't destroy was this computer story-telling machine called Herald. When we went in, to report on the damage, it was still babbling on."

The Bride

The Bride

So you're still teaching down at the old school then? Yeah, thanks I will take a pew this time. Can I say straight up, I'm sorry about last time I came round. Three years almost to the day. Been in Morocco and Spain and India, on the trail like. I'm not rich any more. Three years old these Levis, brought the shirt out there. Have a butchers through the window, no E-Type Jag. Shanks Pony and London Transport, guv.

Must admit, came round that time to come flash, show off, because I remembered something you used to say to us kids in school. What was it? You goes, "You don't get rich by working hard, you get rich by making other people work hard." And I come to tell you that I'd done it on my own. Wasn't true and I knew you wouldn't like it, but I thought I'd make you feel a mug, because you had a prejudice, like, you were always going on at us about how we was working class and would never be loaded.

Nah, not any more. What happened to it? That's what I've come to tell you chief. It's a funny story, but on my mother's life it's true. How did I get poor again? You started it. When? That day three years ago when you showed me that newspaper cutting. You had me well sussed.

Where to start? With Jaswinder, of course. You won't believe this, but it was her made me rich. She gave it me, laid it on me, I'll tell you how in a minute, hang on.

Begin with when I left school. I got these dead beat jobs. Thirty, maybe forty sheets a week. Hey, you remember that half-caste geezer what used to teach us basketball? I met him in a pub down Kew, about two years after I left school. He always pulled tasty birds, didn't he? He comes up to me and he says, "How you doing, Les?"

"Tony," I says.

"Yeah, Tony," he says. Now you wouldn't have made that kind of mistake, would you, as a teacher I mean.

"I'm on the sales side of IPC and Thompson Newspaper groups," I said.

Very impressed he was, till John, remember John, he was with me, says, "Yeah, Tone's got a paper pitch down Camberwell. 'Evening Standard'."

That's what I was doing till I met Carrots, remember her. Turned snobbish, goes with this art school teacher guy, but I got talking to her and her old man was trying to flog jewellery what he made himself and he's looking for lads to fifty-fifty with him for taking it round. So I left the pitch and started in for him.

"Venetian chain, box chain, Boston chain, one, two three four silly money in the store." Diddled him too. Used to go down with his stuff to the Portobello and up the Lock and that kind of market with pseuds buying junk from con artists like me. Struck it rich with Arabs outside hotels who'd give you a twenty and ask you to keep the change for a bracelet worth eighty pence. Not bad.

Slap the box, lay out the bracelets, necklaces, rings, stuff that I got from this geezer and then from my uncle, knocked-off clobber, genuine articles that were as hot as grandma's fresh fried chips, souvenirs that had been on police five, the lot, you name it.

I was making a small whack and having a good time, until I began to realise that being happy is looking hard for what you want, not having what you've got, if you get my meaning. You do? First one. Most people don't. You may have been my English teacher, but you never got me to say things like I meant them, but you were watching me, all those years, so you know what I'm on about.

At least you know who I'm on about. Dead right, guv. I carried a picture of her tattooed on my brain. I thought of her a lot, Jaswinder. What do you expect. I grew up with them Pakis. What else can a poor boy from Southall do? I'll admit it, I was brought up to think white. My dad's a racialist. Still, yeah. When I was young, I mean little, he was always going on about moving because the picture houses had been taken over by Indian films.

It was daft, right, because my old man never saw no films, just watched telly, and my mum used to tell him that the last thing he'd seen was when he took her to Gone with the Wind. And that would start him off.

I knew you used to think I was right prejudiced, but that's because you only joined our school in the fourth year and I was a skin at the time. We had to do it. I'll tell you, I don't think you teachers knew what was going on down there. We was in the minority, right, and it was our country, but you wouldn't allow us to say it. And the Asian kids, they came flash. "Sikhs rule" and all this, and there was so many of them you only opened your mouth if you wanted a taste of knuckle sandwich.

I fancied her something rotten, guv, but in the junior years I didn't let on, because it would have shamed me up bad, guy. But then it started. You think them Asian kids are straight, but what they used to get up to mate was nobody's business. Just like kids anywhere, I suppose. But not Jaswinder. Her dad was mad strict, wouldn't even allow her on to the Broadway. I knew that on Saturdays she'd go shopping with her mum so I used to hang about the cafe, the only white cafe going, and check her on her way there and she'd be shy or cautious or whatever, and hardly say hello when she was with her mum and give you a total blank if she was with her dad, a big turbanned geezer. Enough to frighten the daylights out of you mate. Nah? Out of me, then.

The only Asian kid who hung around with us whites after school was Junaid. He was your favourite, wasn't he? Couldn't do nothing wrong. Butter wouldn't melt in his mouth, except he only got margarine down at the social services where he lived. He only got around with us because he was brought up in care all his life and had to go in with the tough nuts, mostly white kids, down the orphan shop. I know that all of you felt sorry for him, poor kid, teacher's pet. He was nasty, you know. How? I'll tell you. The lads didn't feel sorry for him. He had more money any day of the week than all of us put together, because them kids down that centre used to pull jobs. Remember when they cleaned out the electronics shop by going in through the roof and cutting the plasterboard ceiling? That was Junaid and his mates. He didn't care that it was an Asian shop, he just came all that Asian shit because he wanted sympathy. And he got it too.

Cry? I could have laughed. The girls, they'd wet their pillows for him, if not their knickers. "Aw poor fellow, poor Junaid," the super-runt of Battersea Dogs' Home. Dr Barnardo was invented for him. On my life, he lived on it. And they brought him presents and food and that. He loved it. You could have exchanged my mum, dad and the budgie for half the clobber he got off his tear-jerking violins trip.

All right, that doesn't mean he was nasty, but I didn't much care for him because I knew, from the fourth year up, there was something going on between him and Jaswinder.

And I'd made a fool of myself. On parents' day I followed her around when she was with her dad and chose all the subjects for my fourth year options that she'd chosen. Ended up doing needlework and cookery and bloody

Geography. And Junaid done the same, but you teachers thought he done that to be with the girls because he was a bit like that wasn't he? Not a poof, but kind of soft and wimpish.

When I asked her, at the end of the fifth year whether she was going to the school disco, she replied that her dad was too strict. But she made it in the end and she was necking with Junaid in a dark corner till I couldn't stand it no more. You remember that night? When I smashed up the turn table and you lot had to throw me out? You never reckoned what that was all about did you? A fair idea? Yeah, well, it was because she was kissing him in the corner and I couldn't take it no more so I shouted, "Lights out at the orphanage at eight, homeless mongrels should pack it in."

He came for me and I smashed him one before going for the record he had requested three times. It was Jaswinder stopped him and came between us, and then I was thrown out. I knew I shouldn't have said that but a red haze sort of knocked me out, come in front of my eyes, I couldn't stop myself. She came after me into the winter night.

"Why did you say that to him?" she goes. "You're not like that Tony."

"You know why," I goes.

"You're like my brother," she goes.

"Some fucking brother, I know what you think of whites."

"Not me," she goes, "I'm not . . ."

"Then how come you turn up when you said you wasn't coming when I ask you?"

"My dad, he kicked up a fuss, he wouldn't let me go and I've just come, I don't know what he'll do when he finds out . . ."

I tell you what I did then. I grabbed hold of her and I kissed her. I felt her pulling away and she says, "Tony, please," like something out of a stupid love story and I was thinking it's my only chance, the only time I'd be with her in the dark.

Anyway her dad come round, you remember it? Takes her away and abuses all the teachers.

I went home with my head singing. It was worth it. And as I walked home by the yellow sulphur light, I was that dopey with that kiss I thought "Romeo, Romeo, where art thou," or whatever it was. Pure Shakespeare, guy. But next morning I knew it was no good. Straight up, have you ever loved somebody, I mean fancied her, that it made you sick?

After that I used to hang about netball practice when she was there, the only boy in the gym and I used to hold her purse and her bracelets and that because she didn't want to leave them in the changing room with all the thieving kids about.

I know you knew him well, but I knew him too, guv, Junaid. Remember the time you was reading his story to the class? You'd set us some wimpy English essay on ourselves or something and hardly none of us had done it and Junaid turns up with twenty-eight pages, guy. My Life of Sorrow, he'd called it and even before you took it in for homework, he was handing it round and all the girls were asking him if it was all true and softness like that. She had the bloody nerve to give it to me to read.

"Junaid's story of his life. It should be on telly. You read it, Tony, maybe you'll understand how lonely he is."

I took it off her. Garbage it was. So I told the lads that you'd probably be so chuffed to get some homework back for a change that you'd read it to the class and I filled in them bits. Two pages of filth. Gave it back to Jaswinder, keeping a straight face. Yeah, you remember that, but you sussed it. When she handed it to you, you read it straight, pornography and all till Junaid couldn't stand it no longer and he thought Jaswinder had done the trick on him or at least helped with it and he grabbed the sheets from you and tore them up in front of the class and all the kids were splitting themselves. Junaid came in the next morning blind drunk. He was pretending he'd tried to commit suicide. Bloody joke. And you and Jaswinder fell for it and walked him up and down the corridor to get him over it.

I felt bad, to tell you the truth. But I wished he'd done it. Funny, isn't it?

And he wasn't really Indian, Junaid. He was brought up like us by the social workers and that. He didn't know about their customs like. You remember the next time he began this suicide lark? You don't know what happened. I'll tell you.

I wrote Jaswinder a letter. I finally got up the courage and did it. It was stupid, confessing, but I'd tried everything else. That's why I used to come flash about getting rich one day because I reckoned girls fancy fellers who say they're going to reach the top, any top, and I wasn't good at nothing else. I waited for a reply, but she never sent me one. Instead she came to me at break-time with her mates and she tied this bracelet round my wrist. It was kind of blue and red and gold tinsel, like one of them cloth badges you wear if you support a team. And she gives me a kiss on the cheek.

Then her mate says to me, "It's an Indian custom."

"What's it mean?"

"You got to give her a present first, anything, a bar of Kit Kat."

"Yeah," I said. "I'll get J something."

I got her a teddy bear and I put my gold sovereign round it's neck.

"Now tell me," I said to her and my heart was thumping.

"It mean's you're my brother now and you've sworn to protect me."

"Yeah?" I goes. "How?"

"Like a brother. I really like you Tony, but not in that way, you understand?"

27

I understood, guv. The hollow in my stomach understood. She wants me out of the running. I was a fool to think I could beat it.

But that evening I got up to mischief. I was down the cafe wearing this damn bracelet and Junaid turned up with his thieving mates and they were all taking the mick out of my bracelet, so I told them it was an old Indian custom and Jaswinder had given it me.

"What's it mean?" Junaid said, going serious.

"What's an engagement ring mean, mate?"

He never said nothing but that was when they found him.

She had to explain to him after they'd pumped his stomach out at the hospital and again her dad came and dragged her away and threatened Junaid for messing with his daughter. Right Indian film stuff.

Then school was over and I thought I'd never see her again because I moved down Stockwell with my brother-in-law. I was wrong, of course. I saw her.

It must have been a Thursday night, 22nd of December. I was down an antique market in North London and the lads had lit lamps on their stalls. I didn't have a stall, but I traded off of a lamp of a geezer what sold old records and that. It couldn't have been late, because it was dark early then and when the market packed up at seven or so, we used to go off for a drink. The barrows would be left out in the cold and the fog with their lamps on till the market boys came and dismantled them. I went off to the pub like, I'd done enough trade in the last half hour and the market began to empty. When I finished boozing I noticed the strap for my box was missing, so I thought I'd go back and get it.

The street was littered with cardboard boxes and junk. It was foggy. Dark too. I found my strap and was lacing it to my box when I looked down the street and I thought I saw in the fog a figure of a woman standing by a lit barrow.

The Bride

"Hello," I says to myself, rubbing my hands for cold, "some punter's trading late."

There was no mistaking it. It was a lit barrow piled with show cases and that and I shifted my head and couldn't see no one attending it. But there was this wrapped figure standing in front of it.

"One of the lads left his stuff," I thought, and helpful as ever, I went down the street.

There was no one about and this figure, a lady, turns to me. I thought I'd say something cheeky, like, so I wandered up. I couldn't recall this particular barrow and I would have, 'cause it was in my trade, it was loaded with cases of jewellery, a naked bulb hanging from the wire, plugged in to the junction box on the lampost. The light was throwing shadows on her face so I had to get close up before I saw it was Jaswinder. She was wearing a cape and when she turned to me I saw she was in a saree.

"Stap me dead," I said. "What're you doing here?"

"Looking," she said. "Where's the man who sells these things?"

"Is that all you've got to say to me?"

"I'm in a hurry," she goes.

Then I see she has tears rolling down her cheeks. "I was to be married today, it's my wedding night," she goes.

"Don't spring that on me," I said. "What's the matter? You don't look happy about it."

"Same old story, Tony," she said. "My father arranged a marriage with my neighbour's cousin."

"So why are you alone on a night like this?"

"Alone?" she goes. "There's you."

"Don't talk stupid. What're you doing about it? I thought you'd end up with Junaid."

"He's dead," she said and she began to howl.

"What?"

"And now I'm to be married to a stranger."

29

"When?"

"But I can't find the jewellery I'd like to wear. He's very particular. He is a jeweller and a goldsmith himself."

"Why are you doing it?" I said. I was pleading with her. "This is bloody England. You don't have to marry this geezer. Your dad can't tell you what to do."

"No, he can't," she said, "but I'm to meet my bridegroom and I must have something to wear. Going without jewellery is a kind of pitiable nakedness."

"Didn't your father get you none? How did you end up here?"

"You were here," she said. "I tied a bracelet on your arm three years ago."

"I know," I said. "And I promised. I'll do anything you want, just name it, and if I can do it, you can have it."

"It's England and I can do what I like," she said and her tears seemed to disappear and she laughed.

I don't know whether I was stoned or what, but it was weird. I was thinking to myself that something funny was going on.

"I've got some jewellery. I'm in the trade," I said. "Jaswinder, it's just trinkets, but you can have it if that's all you want."

"It's all I want," she said. "An anklet of gold, a bride should have a golden anklet."

"That's tall," I said. "Not my order," but I opened up my case and dragged out the most expensive chains and that I had. "Maybe not perfect, but it's something. Fourteen carat."

"You were always a bit gone on me, weren't you Tony?"

"Not a bit," I said. "A lot."

"I knew you'd help," she said. "Goodbye Tony."

"Wait a bit," I said, "let me get you a cab. I'll go with you, see you're all right."

But she didn't wait. She didn't even raise a hand. She just

turned and walked into the fog, out of the circle of light. I left my case and I ran shouting after her. I thought she must have dodged down one of the lanes but she wasn't nowhere.

I didn't go home that night. I went to the park, climbed over the railings and walked on the frozen grass and threw stones at the ice on the ponds. I didn't do any selling for the next few days. Just hung about.

Then the next time I was down the same market where I'd met her, I left my box and went for a cup of tea with one of the barrow boys. Left the box on Frank's barrow where he said he'd keep a beady on it for me. Come back and open it to set my stuff out on a mat. Started shouting already, "See what I've got here, darling," all the palaver. Jesus creepers, it caught me short that. You can't guess it. I opened the box and my stuff had gone. Instead there was real hard clobber in it. I couldn't believe my eyes. Solid gold bracelets, earrings with diamonds, rings with sapphires, the metal work done like old designs.

Hullo, I thought, Frank's having a giggle on the side. I looked up at him but he was doing his own trade, poker face.

"Oi, Frank," I said. "What's this lark then."

He didn't know what I was on about. I was that shocked, bits of me froze.

"What're you complaining about," Frank said, cool and wiley.

I figures to myself, he must be trying to pin something on me, he and his mates, fit me up like. So I said I'm taking the lot down the bull-ring, hand the lot in and report my trinkets stolen.

"It's your life," he said, not concerned. He swore nobody had touched that box, though he'd been selling steady and had a crowd.

I took the stuff round to my uncle's who knows gold when he tastes it. He thought they were knocked off too and they looked hot, more carrots than a rabbit's freezer, and the bill would be round eventually, but maybe I could get a reward for the lot. They were too big to keep, he said, so I went down the cop shop and I couldn't tell them the true story so I said I found them. They took my particulars, but the sergeant there he looked at me as though I'd made a run from Cain Hill.

Three months later the cops tell me, the stuff's clean. No reports of it stolen or missing. I could have it.

I couldn't believe it. My uncle takes it down with me to this collector geezer he knows and he says give him three days, he'll trace it. I come back to him and he says it's Indian jewellery, but no mark on it to show who owned it or made it. That's what set me thinking. She done it. Jaswinder. I remembered every word she said that night and it was a jeweller she was being married off to. And I was sure because in the collection there was one of them brother–sister bracelets, only this time in gold and with stones, not a cloth one. But how had she got them to me? I went back to Frank and asked him if there was any Indians hovering about his stall that day.

"Yeah," he says, "Tonto came by. How do you expect me to remember?"

"All right," I said. "No skin off my nose, I'm fuckin' rich."

That's how, guv, that's the story. Flogged all the stuff except the bracelet to this collector and set up shop with my uncle. That's where I got the Jag and the suit you saw me in last time. Spent a year like that. Travelled a bit—Majorca, Costa, you know the circuit. Then I thought I'd find her. I'd go to India and find her even though I was scared. Putting an end to a mystery is always a bit scary for me, I don't know about you. But I made up my mind and I drove down to Southall to check her family. I'd hung about that street a thousand times, walking down past the corner in the evenings when I was still at school, hoping she'd come out. I rung the bell and this Indian lady, oldish come out. I asked for Jaswinder. I said I knew she was in India, but could I have her address?

"No Jaswinder," she says and shakes her head. I couldn't get her to understand what I was after.

Then this little girl in the garden, an Indian girl, comes up and says, "They've gone. That family's gone. My daddy knows them," she says. "That lady doesn't speak English and neither does my mum."

"Where's your daddy?"

"Office," she says.

That's when I come round to you. I thought maybe you'd know. And you told me Jaswinder was dead.

I couldn't live with that. I still had the bracelet. I raced back that evening to Southall and waited for the neighbour, the little girl's father to get home and I stepped up to him out of my Jag.

I asked him about Jaswinder.

"Whole family gone. One year ago. Gone back to India."

He didn't look as though he wanted to talk. I had to tell him some lie. I was thinking on my feet.

"You've got to tell me what you know about it," I said. "Listen, please, I was . . ." I don't know what came into me, I said, "I was her husband."

"Husband?" He looked stunned. "But she was loving muslim boy."

"Which muslim boy? Junaid? I know all about him. Look, we got secretly married but then she went off with this boy she knew from school. I left her alone, I don't know what happened to her then."

He took me inside his house. He was wondering about me, but he was willing to talk after I told him that.

He brought out this newspaper cutting from the local paper. He'd kept it. "Sad business," he said. "Her father was forcing her. Very rich man but too old, he found for her. Jeweller in India. Father was very broken when she kill herself with the muslim boy."

I looked at the date of the newspaper cutting. It was the 22nd of December. The story was dated the 21st.

"This can't be possible," I said. "I saw her on the 22nd."

"You went to funeral? Very sad," he said.

"Look, I wasn't her husband or anything I was just lying to make you tell me about it," I confessed.

"What does it matter," he said. "But you shouldn't tell these kind of lies. You look a decent gentlemans."

"I was her brother," I said, almost to myself and I could see I confused him even more. But I couldn't spend my time sorting him out, if you know what I mean.

I got back home and looked for the bracelet. I kept it in my drawer with my underwear and that. It was gone.

As I went home, I was sure it would still be there, but it wasn't. She would have left me that, I thought, but then I hadn't acted like a brother, I'd been a bit frantic like, I'd blown it.

Homework

Homework

The following story is for dictionary practice.

With these worksheets take a dictionary home from your form cupboard.

The most difficult words in the story are underlined. For each of these words find the correct dictionary meaning and write it in pencil above the word. Then try and read the sentence in which the words occur and try and understand the whole sentence.

Tomorrow in class there will be a spelling test on some of these hard words.

Many civilisations known to man have <u>perished</u>. Under the city of Jerusalem, for instance, there are buried nine cities. Each of these nine cities belong to an age of the human <u>habitation</u> that <u>flourished</u> at one time on that spot. We can learn about the way the people behind these civilisations lived by examining the things they left behind. At different times in human history, people spoke and wrote different languages. <u>Archaeologists</u> have set themselves the task of <u>deciphering</u> these languages, many of which are related to the languages we speak and write today. Some of them are dead languages: which means that no living person knows them. Yet we have some knowledge of how those people lived by <u>codifying</u> their scripts.

Some civilisations, however, have left no trace except

that of legend. The ancient Greeks believed, for instance, that there was a civilisation that had been swept under the sea by natural factors and had continued under water. They called this civilisation Atlantis. Modern scientists have tried to find out when and where Atlantis existed, but without much convincing success.

It is easy, however, to imagine a civilisation of the past which had no written script. The people may and will have talked to each other but will have left no record of their language in written form. Today we feel that the absence of a written script would be a tragedy. We would not, without writing, be able to transmit everything we know to people who come after us. Our sciences would then become extinct.

Imagine, for instance, that twenty five years from the day you read this story, the world is destroyed. It may be destroyed by human agency, such as nuclear warfare, or it may be destroyed, as perhaps was Atlantis, by natural disaster, or in fact by a combination of both.

According to one American scientist, that is not such a remote possibility. He says that our factories are putting out smoke in such density that our planet is under sentence of death. His hypothesis is that the hot smoke rises and forms a layer above the earth. This layer destroys another layer of gas that protects the earth from the full heat of the sun's rays. If the full heat of the sun were to play on the snows of the Arctic and the Antarctic, it would melt the snows of those regions. The melted snow would flow into the oceans and the flood that would ensue would make the flood of Noah look like a puddle in summer rain.

After this flood there will be silence. None of the countries and land that we know will survive, except perhaps the highest peaks in the world. Today those high peaks, such as Mount Everest in the Himalayas in India, are cold and snowbound.

If you imagine a world after this terrible flood, the snow on these peaks will melt. The valleys around them will be flooded and will become part of the oceans and only people who make their way up to the high peaks will survive. They will live on a group of rugged islands surrounded by the sea.

Do these people believe in Gods? Of course they don't. They know very little of what we knew, because they could carry very little of the objects of their <u>environment</u> when they escaped the flood. They are people who have foreseen the destruction of our world. Do they want to build the same world, believe in the same things again? Of course they don't. They want to forget about the science and the industry and the factories and the manufacture that have brought about the world's watery end. So with them they take only the essentials that nature will <u>foster</u>. They take seeds and trees and a few animals.

Their civilisation grows. When the trees mature and yield wood, they build boats. They make tools by striking stone against stone. Their children and their children's children believe in the sunrise and the sunset and the heat of the day and the fresh of the night and are never told about the humans that went before them.

They learn instead the arts of the <u>primitive</u> <u>maritime</u> peoples. How to skin a fish and use its bones as hooks, how to tell the regular ebb and flow of the tides. Through generations they are happy and <u>oblivious</u> of the twentieth century and our factories and our wars and our cities and our schools and our jails and our jealousies.

Amongst one generation of these new people of Everest is a boy called Zal. He goes fishing with his father and the other men of the tribe. He knows all about hooks and bait. Several times in his life he has been dragged off one of the little crafts of the islanders to fight with some monster of the deep, stab it and swim to the surface to ask the assistance of his companions in bringing up his kill from the sea. He swims like a creature with webbed feet, one that can hold its breath underwater for several minutes. He has learnt this skill from childhood, because it is necessary to jump overboard and lure the <u>carnivorous</u> fish by using yourself as human bait.

One day the men in the boat throw Zal over the side and wait for him to rise like a bubble in a bottle of pop. He waves to them, several feet away now, and they throw out the line weighted with a stone that sinks faster than the fish he has killed. It is Zal's task to tangle the body of the fish in this line. It is a great big fish, of a kind that Zal has never seen before. A magnificent catch.

They trail the fish and row back to the island once Zal is safely back in the boat. They pull it up on the beach and require six men to drag the hauling line.

It is Zal's fish. He has the first knife cut. He slits the belly of the fish, cuts its fins and breaks its jaw with a stone. He wants to keep its teeth as souvenirs. The people of his village gather round as he explores the <u>anatomy</u> of this unknown variety of sea monster. Its blood is as wine-red and watery as that of any other fish, but in its belly it contains a strange sack. It is black and thick like the skin of an animal. Zal examines this strange stomach, like an inner stomach. Down one side it has little teeth clamped together which shine like the sun on the waters at dawn. Hard teeth they are too.

"This one has two stomachs and teeth inside its belly too," Zal says.

"Divide the meat," says one of the elders impatiently. "You can keep the inner teeth as a souvenir too."

"I've seen such a monster before," says another elder. "My grandfather captured one. He said they live forever unless a hunter catches them. That one had no second stomach like this."

Zal cuts the rest of the innards of the fish and offers the body to the village. The custom of their village is that they take equal shares of the day's catch.

Then an elder steps forward and says, "Let me have a look at that inner stomach. The fish may be poisonous."

Zal hands the rectangular sack over to the elder.

"Never seen anything like it. I would be very careful about eating the flesh of this one. I feel Zal has caught a poisonous monster. Look at this stomach lining, it's rough and black and oily."

There is a murmur amongst the gathering. A woman speaks out saying that she will not risk taking a piece of Zal's fish home. Others agree.

The gathering moves on to the smaller catches of the day. Zal sits on the ground by his catch. This is unfortunate. It is the biggest fish he has ever caught. Now the people of the village will just leave it there, lying gutted and open like a collapsed tent, its skin resting on the sand, its eye bulgy and misty.

Zal looks down the broken jaw of his prize. The fish has a huge gullet and the inside of its mouth is ribbed like the bottom of a boat, its palate like the white and green and shady red smoothness of some seashells. He gazes long into the fish's mouth. He doesn't notice that one of the elders has come back and is looking over his shoulder. He turns round when he feels a presence.

"The biggest fish you ever caught, isn't it?" the old man says.

"I don't think it's poisonous," Zal replies.

"Dorjay says it is an inner stomach, but it's some kind of octopus that the fish has swallowed, I think," the old man says, and he asks Zal to pass him the black sack. The old man examines it for a few seconds and then throws it on the sand next to the guts of the fish.

"I'm sorry for you boy, but you mustn't be disappointed.

You have long to live. There will be other fish and much appreciation."

"I suppose so," Zal says.

When the old man has gone, Zal turns to the black sack, the inner stomach, or the creature the fish has swallowed whole. He picks it up and looks at its teeth. It is made of a substance he has never before seen in a sea creature. He thinks he'll pry open the teeth. He wrenches at them and pulls them apart, but they are shut tight. He runs his finger along the ridge of the teeth and then he notices that at the end of the row of teeth is a loose one. He pulls at that and as if by magic it unlocks the row of teeth, two by two, right down the row, and the mouth of the creature lies gaping in front of him. This thing is more fascinating than the fish itself, he thinks.

Then it occurs to him that this isn't another fish creature, it is some sort of trap, some sort of net without holes. He has often wondered whether fish have any intelligence as humans do and whether they build traps for each other. But he has always put the thought aside. The shape and form of this trap seems to confirm it. He looks into the sack. If this is a creature, it has no head, no gullet, no stomach. Inside, Zal can see something. The inner skin of the trap is dry and in the bottom of it there is a creature. An animal the trap has caught, Zal thinks. He turns the trap upside down and with a jerk upsets the strange animal on to the sands.

It falls, as though on its mouth, and its jaw stretches open, biting the sands. Zal keeps his distance, wary lest the animal still be alive. He walks closer to it. It is curious, this process of intussusception by which the black creature has ingested this one and the fish has swallowed the black creature.

The creature on the sand lies still, making no move to crunch the sand or crawl away. It looks dangerous. It has a rectangular body, no fins or feet and it looks to Zal as though it is nothing but an open jaw. Zal bends over and

42

puts his head on the sand and looks at the creature. It seems to him to have no teeth but has a thousand white tongues which stretch from its spine. It is like a flat clam. An enormous one, but dead.

Zal wants to make sure. He takes his knife from his belt and pokes the creature. It doesn't move. Now he feels bold and grasps it by its spine and lifts it up. The shell and the tongues flap shut. As Zal lifts it, six or eight of the tongues fall out and strew themselves on the sand. Zal puts the creature down and examines these. They are funny. They are smooth and white and rectangular and have a million black markings on each, markings in regular rows such as Zal has never seen.

Now he picks up the creature and flips its tongues. He runs his thumb along the edges of the tongues. They are as smooth as any skin and they too have markings on them, row upon row. The rows of black markings remind Zal of the regularity of a wheat field, or the rows of tiny fish they lay out all over the beach to dry in the sun.

It is miraculous. On every tongue there are two columns of little black markings. There is an intrinsic design to this creature like nothing he's ever seen. Zal tries to dig his nails into the creature's shell which he now sees is a very dark blue, nearly black, like the ocean on some dark night.

For a few hours he sits looking at the signs on the tongues of this unknown creature. Then he buries it in the sand further up the beach. He will keep his discovery a secret. But how will he find the place where he's buried it again? An idea strikes Zal. He will mark the spot with little signs. He takes his knife out and makes several signs on the spot in the sand. Then he notices that he hasn't buried the loose tongues with the creature. He picks those up. He can bend them easily. He rolls them up, as leaves of the banana tree are rolled around fish to cook them, and he takes them home.

At home he examines the signs and markings on the loose tongues. They may not be tongues, Zal thinks, they may be smaller creatures of the same sort that the bigger creature with the shell swallowed.

Zal keeps his secret and every day when he is on his own he goes and digs up the creature and gazes at it. Then slowly it comes to him. On the tongues of the creature are signs such as he himself made on the sands. The regularity of the signs amazes him. There are darker ones and lighter ones, and soon Zal discovers that they are repeated every so often in one row. It reminds him of the knots that fishermen make in thousands to <u>constitute</u> a net.

It is when he is sitting on the beach with other boys and girls of his age one day and being instructed by the elders in the songs of their forefathers, that a thought strikes Zal like a thunderclap. The thought goes round and round in his head. The boy sitting next to him nudges him.

"Zal."

He looks up at the elder.

"I asked you a question, Zal."

"Yes sir. What was it? I was thinking."

"Day dreaming, child."

The other children laugh.

"I asked you to repeat the song you memorised yesterday."

"Yes sir."

"Well?"

"I've forgotten, sir."

"Forgotten? I don't understand, Zal. Do you forget to eat or to take your share from the day's catch?"

"Once I go away, I forget," Zal says.

"That's no crime. But couldn't you have asked someone else? The words are easy. It's part of your homework."

"There must be some other way of remembering, sir," Zal says.

"What other way, child, except constant repetition and passing on what you know so that knowledge may be shared."

"Well, sir, I was just thinking. If we had a sign for all the words we speak, one different sign for each word, then we could . . ."

"Yes," says the elder, "and if we had a name for every fish that lived in the sea we wouldn't have to catch them, we could call them out by shouting their names."

The rest of the children laugh.

"No fishing trips for you for a week," the elder says. "Now listen while I ask someone else to repeat yesterday's song. Your mind is not on your work. Or it's like a net with larger holes than the fish."

For a week Zal isn't allowed on to the boats. He feels hurt by the punishment. He makes sure he has learnt the song by doing exactly as he had suggested to the elder. While sitting on the sands, he makes little signs for the words of the song and the next day he comes back and finds the signs in the same order.

The more Zal thinks about it, the more he is convinced. Every day he looks at his captive creature of the tongues. If by some chance, he thinks, by some design, the signs on the flat tongues of the creature have been arranged there by some creature like himself capable of making signs in the sand and each of the signs . . . But no, it is too improbable to even contemplate.

Though he puts this thought out of his head, Zal still examines the signs in the creature for their regularity. In a few months' time he finds, by carefully tracing the signs on the sand next to him as he leafs through the tongues, that there are about seventy signs. Thick ones and thin ones, slanting ones and vertical ones. Soon Zal is able to copy on the sands whole rows of the signs. But he can never know what they mean. When he copies the signs in the sand with

45

his knife, or carves them on palm leaves, he notices that he can never get them as straight and neat as the rows of signs on the creature's tongues. No matter how hard he tries, all he can make are squiggly imitations.

That's why they couldn't have been made by creatures like me, Zal thinks. They are too regular. And yet on the loose tongues that he found, eight of them, there are squiggly signs like Zal's. They are inscribed above other signs with dark black lines under them. Slowly Zal learns to imitate all the signs on these loose tongues. They begin like this:

Homework

The following story is for dictionary practice.

With these worksheets take a dictionary home from your form cupboard.

The most difficult words in the story are underlined. For

And then at the end, on the blank part of the tongue, are these squiggly signs, definite indications that someone like Zal could have made them: *Stuff this, this is boring*.

The Mandarin Exam

The Mandarin Exam

I did it for a bet. A mate of mine bet me fifty quid, his life savings. I didn't have fifty quid so I had to win. The games hall was full of desks and we had to take our shoes off when we filed in because the teachers were afraid that we'd damage the wooden floor. *They* kept their shoes on. There were a hundred and fifty of us in our year and the desks were separated into one row for the O levels and five rows for the CSEs. When the Headmaster came in and took his stop watch from his pocket, and after the teachers had handed out the paper and stuff, it all become quiet. It was English.

I knew the stories backwards. I was good at this sort of stuff and who knows, I might have done stacks of questions, but I had to win the fifty quid and there wasn't any point passing CSE English anyway. When they all got their heads down and started writing, I pulled out my snuff box in which I kept a bit of smoke and took some RIZLA papers from my pocket and started licking them and putting them together. I must confess, I felt a bit nervous doing it, because the teachers were watching like cats surveying mice.

The English teacher comes past my desk and leans over and he says, "What're you doing?"

"Marking time," I says. I knew he'd understand what I was talking about.

He takes the RIZLA pack from out my hand and scoops

up the snuff box after having a look into it and then walks off.

"Get on with it," he says.

Now I deliberately hadn't brought a pen. I picked up the question paper. I was dying to look at it, see if it was easy and what I was missing, but I sat back and tore it up. Back he rushes.

"What the hell do you think you're doing, Spiggy?"

"Tearing up the paper, sir."

"I see. Have you got nerves or something?"

"Steel nerves," I says.

"Don't you want to do the paper?"

"What do you reckon, pal?"

"All right," he says and without argument goes and gets the Headmaster. Now the rest of the kids are looking round. The word has spread, see, that I'm going to make my protest.

Headmaster comes up. Kids look round and there's a murmur in the hall.

"Get on with your work," he says in a voice raised to room temperature, then he leans over and asks me if I'd like to go outside and have a quick smoke under supervision and he'd see that I could come back and do the exam in five minutes.

"I don't want to do the exam, sir, I told Mr Scott and he didn't want to know."

"I see." He rubs his jaw.

I thought he'd do his nut, but he just strolls about near my desk.

"No use disturbing the rest," he says. "You can go."

"Thank you, sir," I says.

"But you disappoint me lad," he says.

"My principles," I says.

"Does your dad know?"

"He'll soon know."

The rest of the kids are getting on with it.

The Head asks me to go to his office to explain.

I go to his office and he says, "What do you want to do in life? You know you can't stay on in the sixth form without qualifications."

"I want to be a writer," I says.

"So you tear up your English paper?"

"That's right."

"Not logical, is it?"

"More logical than what they teach us, sir." I wanted to remain polite. He asks me to sit down and say what I mean.

"You didn't like the books you did?"

"Yeah, I liked them."

"Then what was the problem? Didn't you know any of it?"

"I don't know, didn't look, did I?"

"Curious," he says biting his lip and looking like he was thinking of something else.

"But it's all lies. We was doing this story, sir, it's called The Loneliness of the Long Distance Runner."

"Yes, I know it."

"In this story there's this kid what goes to borstal for thievin' and his dad's dead and he hates the people what keep the laws, like, teachers and borstal governors and that and he only finds his freedom when he's allowed to go on cross-country runs."

"And so?"

"He's like me, except I can't run, got asthma."

"So you identified with him. His name's Smith in the story isn't it?"

"Yes, sir. He has to run this race for his borstal and the posh geezers are watching and he loses the race because he don't want to win for them."

"I remember," he says. "And what's that got to do with your not doing the exam?"

"I'm a bit like that, sir. I got a good imagination, I reckon, and I don't see the point in doing the exam. See, Mr Scott he loves that story, right, but if any of the kids in his class behaves like that he don't like it."

"I get the point."

"Exams and that, where's it going to get you? A job? I don't want a job. I just want the loot that goes with it. Nah! I don't want that trip, it's a trap."

"A bit of a philosopher are you Spiggy?"

"Yes," I said, 'cause I didn't know what else to say. "Can I go, sir?"

"Sure, when you please," he says, rotating in his swivel chair. "But I'd like to tell you something before you do. Do you have the time? I don't suppose we'll see you again."

"I'll drop in," I says.

"It may help you with your writing."

"I want to write the truth," I says.

"We all do. But I want to tell you a story."

"Is it true?"

"Maybe."

"Go on then, sir. I like stories."

I don't know to this day why he took the time but this is what he told me.

"It's set in China," he begins, and he walks about the room and he looks out of the window. "We must have failed with you. This story, though, is about a man who failed exams, except that I don't know the ending."

"What's the good of it, then?" I asks.

"You might find some good in it. It starts in the thirteenth century A.D. In China they used to call all their high officials Mandarins and before you became a full Mandarin, you had to do this examination. It was a most curious exam. It didn't have any time limit and it didn't have any subject as such. The person doing the exam was allowed to come and go from the exam hall and take as long as he liked. There was only one question on the paper. You know what it was? It was always the same. It said 'Write what you know'. Now that wouldn't suit you, would it? That's right. You wouldn't know where to start.

One fellow, a young man much like you, but of his time, you understand, did the exam, as far as the records show, four times. The first time he took the exam was when he was sixteen, then when he was thirty-two, the third time when he was sixty-four and the last time when he was a hundred and twenty-eight years old. They lived to a ripe old age in those days.

His name was Wu Fan'tsi. And he had a very severe tutor. The first time he was asked write all you know, he started by looking and listening. He described the pen he was writing with in great detail, the grain and shade of the paper on which he wrote, the room, the shape of his hand as it wrote. That took him eight months. Then he wandered out and described the sky as it changed from day to day, the birds that flew past, the trees and the inclination and shape of every leaf on the trees he could see. He noted the sounds that came to him, the feel of the gravel underfoot and the exact pitch of every syllable that made up the speech of the people with whom he talked. That took him eight years.

He was determined to pass that exam, no matter how long it took him. He began describing the features of his tutor and the other disciples who came now and then into the examination room where he sat. He filled book after book with his answer. He was now thirty one years old.

Surfaces. That's all you really know, he thought, and he scribed on from day to day, week to week and year to year. Hard work? I should have thought so. And then at thirty-two, he gave it up and he went to his tutor and his tutor asked him if he had completed the exam. He had to admit he hadn't. Every new moment would give him new impressions to describe. His tutor smiled. Wu Fan'tsi said he was dissatisfied with the years he had spent describing things. Things were dead and surfaces were always changing. He'd now dedicate himself to describing changes. Yes, he agreed he had failed.

Straight away he started his second attempt on the exam. He abandoned the books he had filled and started afresh, describing his life. One book was dedicated to the days he had spent and how he had grown. The next book was dedicated to the history of China and all the known world. At that time they thought, perhaps they still do, that China was the centre of the world, and he wrote for sixteen years on the story of the Middle Kingdom—which is what they used to call their country.

He wouldn't read any books, but he'd wander about between writing, sometimes absenting himself from the exam room for years. He got married and had children. He didn't need to work, because the mandarins all came from families whose wants were supplied. He just observed and he wrote. He has left us a very boring but very long history of China, of his own life, of the lives of the other people he came into contact with. More than that, he wrote a geography, a rather brief one, about the changes of season and vegetation in the country he knew.

By the time he thought he'd finished, he was fifty-nine years old and he was dissatisfied with the answer he had written. So he went to his tutor and he said, 'Great keeper of our ancestor's secrets, I want leave to try this examination again. I have given my life to knowing how things are and how things change, but it doesn't seem a wise course to me any more.'

His tutor smiled.

Wu Fan'tsi knew he had failed for the second time and began to wander in the world once more. When he was sixty-four years old, he came back. He said he was ready to try the exam again. His tutor gave him leave.

Wu Fan'tsi sat down at the exam desk and he called for paper.

'This time,' he announced, 'I'm going to write all I know and my knowledge is in the dreams of human beings.'

He was an old man now and new disciples had come in to listen to him. They had all heard of Wu Fan'tsi the exam-doer, and they thought to themselves that his brain had gone soft with all the years he had spent writing. But still he wrote.

This time he wrote of things to come. He wrote, and this is quite remarkable, for the thirteenth century at least, that China would no longer be the middle kingdom, that all human beings would be equal one day, that they would fly and go to the stars and that they would put wanting things and being hungry and thirsty and diseased behind them. He dreamt some dreams and made some prophecies that few people have made to this day.

And after twelve years of writing, he took the thesis to his tutor.

'Dreams and visions,' his tutor said. 'And what will become of the gods and of the souls of our ancestors?'

The two old men confronted each other and looked in each other's eyes. The young disciples gathered around.

'That I don't know, so I didn't write it,' said Wu Fan'tsi.

'Dreams,' the old tutor said and he was a wise one. And he proceeded in front of the crowd to ask Wu Fan'tsi a hundred questions to which he could only reply that he didn't know. Then his tutor smiled and Wu Fan'tsi kow-towed, which means bowed very low with his head on the ground and he took his book of predictions and dreams and he said to his tutor, 'I have not said what I know, the question is not answered.'

It was the third time he had taken the exam. He was now seventy-six years old. He had twenty children. His wife had died, his children were grown up and had gone into the world thinking their father a dreamer and had ten children each of their own and some of those children had children.

'I have taken the least time to write the answer on this third attempt,' said Wu Fan'tsi as he left his tutor, 'because life is long and prophecy is short and dreams come to an end when you wake.'

Wu Fan'tsi went away. He travelled beyond China and lived, it is said, with the Indian people and then with the Arabian people and then with the white people beyond the bounds of the civilised world. He listened to their stories. He found out that the Middle Kingdom was not the middle kingdom at all and that no one knew where the edge of the earth lay. He found out that the Indians worshipped gods with many heads and many arms and finally worshipped no gods at all, that it was all play. He found out that the Arabs had a god whom they were willing to kill for, that white people burned witches at the stake and believed in a god who was born of a woman who had never known a man.

After many years he came back to the world of his people. Then he walked in China and worked as a farmer, as a lifter of loads, as a beggar man with a rice bowl, as a soldier sent to far lands, even though he was over a hundred years old, as a buyer and seller of things in the market-place, as a burier of sacred eggs, as an attender of graves, as a singer who earns his living when he doesn't have a sore throat, as a catcher of fish, as a builder of houses, and many other things. Then he thought he was ready. He came back to his tutor.

'I am ready to do the exam again.'

'You don't have the years left in you,' his tutor said, 'and I don't have the years left in me to see that you have reached wisdom.'

'It won't take long,' Wu Fan'tsi said. 'I need but a few seconds.'

The tutor called for paper and a pen and Wu Fan'tsi

bowed his head to the ground again and then he wrote just one word, the answer to the question 'Write all you know'.

The tutor took the paper from his hand and he didn't smile when he read the word. He embraced Wu Fan'tsi. That was the fourth time he had taken the exam and this time he had passed."

"No one knows what happened to him after that. That's the story. Do you like it?"

The Head went to the cabinet and took out two glasses and a bottle of sherry. I reckon he was more pleased having told his story than I was hearing it.

"It's all right," I said, "but what's it got to do with me not doing my exam?"

"It's a true story," he said and poured out the sherry. "I presume you drink."

"I don't reckon it is," I said. "True, I mean," and I looked beyond the specs into the Head's eyes.

"Why do you think that?"

"Because, well, I mean, he could have lived that long, but people don't act like that, they don't do what stories say they do."

"That might be so, but they teach you something, stories."

"Don't know," I said.

"Think about it when you're a hundred and twenty-eight years old," he says.

"I know what the word is already. What he wrote on the piece of paper and passed the exam, but if I'd written that, I'd have failed."

"That's life," said the Headmaster.

Batty and Winifred

Batty and Winifred

Mr Batt first noticed that something was very wrong when, on the last double period of a Thursday afternoon, he was in the process of teaching what they called "English" to his pet hate of a fourth-year class. Thursday afternoons were difficult for any teacher and with this particular class called 4I, even Monday morning would have been no picnic for Mr Batt for whom most mornings were beginning to be trials and most afternoons torture. It hadn't always been like this. He had taught for twenty-two years. Times had changed.

At first, in a still vivid past of order with "incidents" (oh dear, yes, there were incidents!), St Paul's and All Angels had been a quiet school in a subdued though working-class area of Camberwell, London. Then the teddy boys began to come. At least that's what Mr Batt and the newspapers called them. He was young then, could cope, could hope. They called themselves rockers. They wore forbidding leather jackets, studded belts (clearly not for the purpose of holding their trousers up) and navvies' boots. His little joke was that the place should now be called Screw-balls and Hell's Angels. No one laughed at his little joke. He was an advanced one in the staffroom at the time. There were none of these young biddies out of illiterate colleges, flaunting their legs in mini-skirts and unfairly taxing the boys' fantasies and good manners. Outrageous. And now they were all around him in diaphanous dresses, in T shirts and jeans, women who wore no brassieres and knew no etiquette.

Then the blacks came. Mr Batt tried hard to keep abreast of the times. He even read the books that his girlish Head of Department thrust upon him when she took over from kindly Mrs Snoraway; strange books on Jamiacan dialect, the religions of the coloured children and books which seemed to say that the little animals must be allowed to do as they pleased. And still Mr Batt kept his end and humour up. He learnt from the children that the rough fellows with knotted unkempt hair, the sort that would have been clapped in leg-irons if they had as much as dared to take one breath of free air in his native Hartlepool some thirty or maybe even twenty years ago, were known as Rastafari. His joke about 4I, innocently named after the year and the room in which they began each fresh day, was calling them Rasta-four-I. Oh, they laughed the first time. There was a sprinkling of troublesome coloured among them and Mr Batt knew it made them feel acknowledged.

No use, oh no use at all, trying to drum through their reluctant heads the niceties of English, the language of Keats and Chaucer. What would they make of it through their pathetic clamour? But *she*, the Head of Department, *she* with the long sharp nose and rat-like eyes, *she* who fawned to the Head and talked nonsense with the Inspectors, *she* had approached him one day.

"Mr Batt, can I call you Harry, it's time the fourths learnt similes and metaphors. Don't call them that, tell them they are comparisons, that one thing is like another, they'll have fun with that . . ."

Grandmothers swallow their pride and suck eggs, thought Mr Batt. He'd stopped himself from replying that he knew about the English language and teaching it when she was shitting her nappies. But oh no, that wouldn't do. *She* was authority.

Mr Batt just smiled. *She* could tell him that. *She* could impress all the beardies and weirdies who called themselves

English teachers, but she (and they) would never find the two hundred and sixty-three dictionaries that Mrs Snoraway had left in his charge. He had locked them away. She had asked for them, but Mr Batt had pretended he didn't know what *she* was talking about. The only way she could get them was to dig in his pockets, trouser pockets, and get the key. What did she want, similes, metaphors . . .

He tried. They wouldn't listen. So, as he often did nowadays, he stepped to the blackboard, took up a position with his head raised like an operatic soprana in full flow and launched. Oh they wouldn't understand it, not in a million years, but the person in the next class would hear his voice above theirs.

"Metaphor is the chief weapon of a poet. He flashes it like a sword. The rhythm of similarity, dancing through creation . . . the unseeing eye is forced in a flash, an epiphany, to see lovers as compasses, lives being turned out as lights and candles are, hearts being broken like bread . . ." It was no good. They could shout louder. Tracey and Sharon, God help them and their ugly names, were reading some trash in a duet. The coloured boy Homer was throwing spit darts at the ceiling. Johnson was drooling out of the window and the nasties were playing cards. What if *she* walked in? So he shouted. He gave up metaphor and then it happened.

The shouting trick usually worked. They would be silent for an instant and he would have to produce the next trick.

"Rasta-Four-I!" he shouted. And the class was hushed, but hullo? For a moment, a flash, Mr Batt saw grey and when his eyes cleared he could swear that all the children, all benighted thirty of them, had coloured faces, negro faces and the bushy rag-doll black hair, the locks of those . . . these . . . people!

Blinking clears the sight, resets the mind. It did. It was gone. There was the coloured girl, Winifred, grinning cheekily at him from the front row. There were the boys, white as custard, playing cards. Thank Christ it had passed. And the girl Winifred . . .

Bad customer. The root of it. He had had to see the Head about her the previous day. And she was grinning and her friends were grinning. This girl had broken . . . oh no, what she had done was write the most abject filth in her essays. At first he hadn't known if it was a new style that *she* perhaps would approve of, but when she did it again and again and concealed notes to him in her English folder, he had been forced to take action. Those words! Only when he was in the RAF had he allowed himself to say or think such words. She had cost him. Out of his mind. He must put her grinning, stupid face out of his mind.

Saved by the bell. Mr Batt put his chalk into his Golden Virginia tin and walked stoopingly, carefully, to the staffroom. With never a begged pardon the animals rushed past him, brushed past him. Mr Batt found his favourite chair in the staffroom and sank in it. The colour went from his face. He brushed the few strands of hair that he placed with care to conceal his baldness on to the front of his head (what did these monstrous kids call him? They had a running developing joke; What would Batt be called if he went to Germany? Herr Batt, Ha, ha, ha! Why was Batt late? He went to a bald meeting. And, What does he do after school? He goes skate-balding. All half-baked puns), but he couldn't concentrate. A voice like the hum of a top, a yo-yo-yo-yo sound, kept speaking to him from inside his skull. Then *she* was upon him.

"You don't look too hot."

"I'm cool," he said and the wind swept through his sweater.

"Coffee?" and she was gone.

"Who let those kids into the bloody staffroom?" Mr Batt boomed. There were a few teachers who looked around and there were some pupils whom the drama-wallahs had gathered round them, damn their souls. Strictly speaking, they were not allowed beyond the foyer, but who spoke strictly nowadays? He would have said "gone to pot" if they hadn't changed the meaning of that too.

"Kids in the bloody staffroom," he said again and opened his eyes to glare and they were there. Five kids: baby goats with legs splayed, gathered round the drama teacher and when he looked away, the tables and walls of the staffroom, running crimson and dripping, covered.

Oh my good Jesus. Mr Batt cupped his eyes with both palms. *She* was hovering above him again, with her foolish concern and her cup of coffee.

"You don't look at all well, Harry, like you've seen a ghost."

"They are driving me batty," said Mr Batt, hoping to humour her. It would pass. And he stretched a black, webbed, fretted wing, oily and veined, downed with piles of ugly hair to take the coffee cup. He was up on his feet wiping the stains off her skirt with his handkerchief. She stepped back as though she thought he was trying to feel her through his handkerchief and lifted the spilt mug.

"Sorry, awfully," he said and he thought, It's what I saw, good god have pity, it's what I saw.

"Was it hairy?" she was asking. "Four-I? Are they getting out of hand?"

Mr Batt sank back in his chair. She sat next to him mopping her skirt.

"You're not letting that Winifred business bother you are you? I thought after our little chat . . ."

"No," said Mr Batt. How dare she? "Some of these coloured kids can't swallow the poetry."

She bit her bottom lip. She was going to be tactful in her reply. And Mr Batt saw the joke. This time he expected it. He saw the pupils in the corner again. Yes, they were kids, goaty and coloured every unthought colour of the rainbow, red, pink, violet, blue, indigo, and they were vomiting reams of it, chewed up words of poetry. And behold, he had to laugh.

"You're better," she said.

He looked at her and it came back to him. Her long nose; it was as they said.

"Blooming Concorde," Mr Batt said. And it came to pass that the supersonic plane looming out of her face from under the glare of her ratty eyes, began to sprout flowers. A touch of spring in a mechanical world.

"It's these silly words I use. You wouldn't call people coloured," Mr Batt said.

"Oh, right," she said. Stupid Concorde. Silly little bitch.

She looked puzzled now. His voice had drawn the attention of the other teachers. "One must have such respect for words," he said. He stood up and walked out of the staffroom with his briefcase. Their eyes would stare, could stare. He knew they were recalling his shame.

It had started innocently enough. He was just doing his job. He had asked 4I to write an essay on themselves. They could write about their hobbies, their families . . . all that. Winifred's essay was damnable cheek. It started off well enough, with her family and her pet dog and then it suddenly said "If you really want to know, you dream doll, I am fourteen and that's under age for what you want to do to me. School subjects? You darling wally, I don't like them, I only come to school to see you."

Mr Batt scratched out those lines and he gave her two out of ten and he said nothing in class, just swallowed hard when he gave her folder back to her and she stood in front of him with her hip unbalanced and gum in her mouth. The next time it was worse. He had asked them to write about their chosen future.

Winifred wrote, "I want to be your sexy doll. I have had it in fifty different ways with ten different men. I want it

with you. All of those boys were only practice for you . . ."
And the essay went on to describe the ways in which she had
had it. Mr Batt's glasses nearly fell off. His red pencil
dropped. His breathing became thick as he read twice
through this terrible, terrible filth. The bloody cheek of it.
He read it six times before he remembered that the liver was
in the oven. It was burnt. He went to bed hungry.

Winifred didn't give him any indication the next day. He
had torn the pages out of her folder. He took no action. But
he watched her. She was a comely wench. Coloured, with a
cheekily protruding bottom on a lithe body that rose from
tattered shoes through thin calves and athlete's thighs. And
the broad mouth with the smile and eyes that laughed with
it. Oh god have mercy on me, a bachelor and a sinner, but
that was in my RAF days. Must I be punished now?

The next time he took their folders in there were no
answers from Winifred on the poem they had done, but a
letter which said that she thought he was gorgeous (how
they fail to choose their words) and that she wanted it, it, it.
With him. The letter said what they would do. She was
carrying this too far, but Mr Batt carried the letter with him
to the launderette. He read it again and again as his underwear rotated and sploshed. He said nothing. A third and a
fourth letter arrived. They made dirty suggestions. Suggestions that Winifred meet him, Batt, after class and that they
would go away in his free periods to the caretaker's shed
where the spare desks were stored.

How could he ask her to stay after class and ask her how
she meant all this? Oh, yes, she was beautiful, but she was
young, so young to be so brazen and mind you, they came
as bold as brass these days.

Still Mr Batt said nothing and did nothing and after class a
succession of Winifred's friends came and asked him if he
had liked the work they had written for him the previous
day.

My job, my career, thought Mr Batt. He had heard of this kind of thing. He had read in the papers about teachers being dismissed for tampering. Tampering? A fourteen year old girl and fifty-five year old man with a bald patch? Just a patch, yes, just a patch.

The next time he saw her he thought: "How sweet and lovely dost thou make the shame, Which like a canker in the fragrant rose, Doth spot the beauty of thy budding name." Shakespeare. Yes. That was his business. Not this girl. His business was language. I lie in bed, he thought and thrill over the metaphors of Keats and Swinburne. I have said it so often. I even told the English department meeting, the day they were carrying on with their nonsense about broken duplicating machines, that I couldn't be expected to care, I whose finger tips tremble as they turn a page, I to whom something unmistakeable happens in the forehead when I come to a revelation in a beautiful line . . . The beardies and weirdies were embarrassed and *she* coughed and changed the subject.

She can't even express herself, Mr Batt thought, wrestling to put her out of his mind. And he took up his red pen and he gathered her letters and he corrected every sentence and marked it up for spelling mistakes. No grammar. No sentences at all, but something in her stumbling, fumbling words gave me cramp in the thigh. In the thigh? Mustn't we be exact? How am I moved by this nonsense? And he knew it by heart:

"Harry, lover, I want it 'cos mmmm I betcha, you use Brut aftershave."

Pap. It was pap. Dangerous pap.

Mr Batt resolved to see the Headmaster. Lay it before him. But not the letters. He couldn't show him those. He'd have a word. So in the morning, after his three Weetabix (Weeatbices, should it be? Ha, ha) he checked to see that the letters were safely in the drawer in which he kept his carefully ironed shirts and set off for school. He made an appointment with the Head and laid the truth, most if it, before him. This girl had conceived a passion for him. She had written, very poorly, to him. He had to consider his job. He didn't want her parents to find out that she was thinking and writing in this way. He didn't want a court case.

The Head was understanding. He asked if he had told any other teachers. He asked if any of Winifred's friends knew.

Mr Batt waited around that evening and pretended that he wanted to consult the caretaker about keys until he saw Winifred enter the Head's office. Then Winifred came out and went back in with her two friends. Then the secretary came out and called someone from the staffroom. *She* came out and two boys from 4I were called in and then another teacher, their form teacher, was summoned by the Head.

And when ten of them were crammed into the Head's study, Mr Batt thought he heard the laughter break out. It came down the corridors at him like an overfed animal, lazy and slobbering and yet jaunty. They laughed. Winifred's shrill laugh and the boys and the form teacher and then *she* laughed. It sounded to Batt as though they were holding their guts and rolling about the flecked carpet of the Head's study.

Somewhere in his mind Mr Batt had told himself that he would wait for the interview to be over and then he would go up to Winifred and his eyes would tell her that he didn't mean to tell on her. That he hadn't shown the Head the letters, he still had them. Reassure her. She would know it was impossible. And she would give him a glance as the lady in the Lyons Corner House had done in 1953, a glance that could have lasted hours. And his very eyes would tell her that three times fourteen was still less than fifty-five and that her mother—he'd seen her, at parents' evenings—she was young enough to be his daughter, and couldn't they just, perhaps . . .

But now the laughter was no mere lazy animal, it was a stampede. He was trampled underfoot and he ran to the staffroom for his briefcase. Too late. *She* came up. She glanced at him and below the window he could hear the boys and the girls from 4I, the ones who had been in the Head's study.

"He's fuckin' mad, old baldy."

"It was a flippin' joke, he shouldn't get his knickers in a twist."

"Gawd, he didn't fall for it, he bloody went for it."

And a penny dropped through a rusty slot. How betrayed, my Jesus. And looking out of the window he saw Winifred and her friends. They weren't laughing. He thought Winifred was blinking to hold back tears. Oh lord, what have I done? But the next morning he came back to school and carried on as normal and it was a Thursday and the staff were all laughing at him behind the palms of their hands, those women in their floppiness and those men in tight jeans with their explosives all contoured and showing.

They misunderstood him. He had gone to the Head to complain about the lack of literacy and grammar amongst the fourth years. Of course he had mentioned Winifred. She was probably the worst. Bad morality, bad writing. It was all the same. So he said when *she* came up talking about "some little affair with Winifred".

That was the afternoon it began. He thought perhaps it would go away.

"Have you got the keys to the dictionary cupboard in your pocket?" she asked as he hurried to flee.

"Bats in my belfry, more like," he said as he slammed the staffroom door and he heard the chimes and felt the flutter in his brain, the flapping of vile creatures which made his ears hum and his eyelids vibrate.

He saw her from a distance, beyond the school gates, at the bus-stop he used.

"Mr Batt," she began.

Have you been weeping, my angel, he thought. And he said aloud: "The lily I condemned for thy hand," and immediately the black hand was was a sliver of white and still he walked on.

"I want to talk to you," Winifred said.

"You're a bitch," he said and his eyes saw red and through the red came the growl and the snarl and the bared teeth. But it might have been that it was a soft red tongue and a low switching tail, a dark nose nuzzling up to his fingers. He didn't know any more. No bus. He wouldn't wait. Mr Batt ran. Yes, he ran.

I must say nothing, he thought and he said nothing as he turned the key, panting, in his door. He said nothing as he switched on the news, nothing as he cooked supper, nothing as he picked the fluff of his dressing-gown off his bedroom slippers.

He should have gone in with his brother into the timber business.

"The whole thing stinks," he said aloud, and his nostrils were drowned in the smell of dead flesh, rotting grain, gutted fish, crockery with fungus on it . . .

So he said aloud to whatever power of language it was, "I don't mean this place, I mean the affair. Winifred. These people have reduced me to I don't know what. And *she*, ever since she came I saw the school going downhill . . ." and there he stopped.

He could see the school buildings on skids, rolling down some long slope to destruction.

"No," he said. "Not downhill, it's just gone to the dogs." He wondered what would happen. It made him smile.

Conscious of his power he became frivolous. "My love is

like a red, red rose," he said and the scent was in his chest.

"The forbidden apple," he said and he ate it for dessert. Sweet and a tinge of sour.

"They can all fuck off," he chuckled and he could see them all somewhere, doing it, as Winfired said, in a place called "off".

"A pun my word," he said.

Mr Batt knew he had the living power of metaphor. He knew he had not much else. What he thought affected nothing. What he said could shake the world. There would be hands powerful enough to shake it like a baby's rattle if he gave the word. He wouldn't. He would ask the nurse for three teaspoons of sugar in his tea, please.

He stirs the tea. With it she gives him two envelopes. One is a card from the whole of form 4I. It says: "Get well soon, sir. You know the latest one? What do they give him for breakfast at the hospital? Bald eggs. Hunh, innocent enough, thinks Mr Batt. Guilty.

The other card says: "Please get well soon," and it has some cheap sentimental nonsense, copied from a pop-song no doubt.

"Listen to the whisper of the time and the tide, that's the way baby, that's the way I cried, 'cause love's a triangle with only one side."

Mr Batt puts the tea down and reads it over and over again.

"Utter trash," he says and he reads it aloud.

"That's the way baby, that's the way I cried, I wish you were here, right by my side.

"You see, I am. I am uttering trash."

And there's no comparison, but he waits.

The Fifth Gospel

The Fifth Gospel

When the professor disappeared, two detectives came to interview me. I was then a very poor student in a very cold room at the top of a very old house in Cambridge. My landlady knocked on my door. I was the only 'foreign' lodger she had ever had and she acted as though she knew all along that one day the police would call. The detectives asked me questions on the doorstep and she stood in the hallway and listened over my shoulder. I told them nothing beyond the fact that I had delivered a manuscript to the professor the day before.

"What was in it?"

"I have no idea."

"You were the last person to go in to his rooms."

"I came out again, didn't I?"

They weren't satisfied, but they went away. I had promised the professor that I would say nothing to anybody. The police left me alone for a few days. The story of his disappearance broke in the newspapers. I kept my silence. I break it now for one reason only. The man to whom I gave that promise no longer exists.

He was called Professor James Jardin, archaeologist, theologian and devout Chrsitian. I met him in my first few weeks at the University when at the age of nineteen I came to Britain for the first time from India. And that I suppose is where the story starts, except to say that my grandfather was a great collector of old books and manuscripts. I remember very little about him, but the odour of old pages still wreathes his memory.

He spent most of his day among his books. The rest of the family were not allowed into his room, but from the time I could crawl I was given the licence to explore it. He would seat me on his knee and take down some volume and read it to me. When I was three or four, I can remember him reading aloud to me obscure passages from Persian manuscripts, political tracts in German, Urdu poetry, anything that he happened to be delving into, even though it made not a whit of sense to me. Which of course didn't matter. It was the expressive drone of his shaking voice I remember.

When my grandfather died, my father sold his collection and it was packed into the chests and carried away. All that was left of him was his steel cupboard with a few pin-striped suits with twenties' lapels, a gold tie-pin, an ornamental silver watch and chain, a Parsi prayer book and cap, and a medal he'd won in the First World War as a stretcher bearer in the British–Indian army. All this was kept for me by my mother till I grew up. And with it a manuscript and a note.

The manuscript was bound in brown leather. It had no title. My grandfather had sealed it by stitching it with wire and stamping the molten sealing wax with his own thumb-print. The note was addressed to my father. It said: 'Only one man in the world is to see the content of these pages. I want this manuscript conveyed by hand by trustworthy persons to Professor James Jardin of Queens' College, Cambridge University in England. He knows something of what is in it. If anybody else asks for this manuscript by description, it is not to be given to them. Deny its existence.'

His wish was not forgotten, even though the manuscript lay in the cupboard till I was on my way to England. My mother gave it to me and was glad of the opportunity to fulfil the old man's wishes after twelve years. My father treated them as excessive and eccentric and wondered aloud whether we shouldn't sell the manuscript to a museum if it was worth a few rupees.

How that document came into my grandfather's possession I did not know. I carried it with me dutifully and in my first few days in England was so preoccupied with learning how to deal with slot meters and strange people that I neglected it. I mentioned Professor Jardin to my tutor and told him that my grandfather who was a collector had carried on some sort of correspondence with him.

"Jardin?" he said, sitting at the piano and asking me if I knew any Chopin. "Poor old boy, on his last legs. You can look him up at Queens'. Getting a bit soft now. Brilliant fellow."

I wrapped the manuscript in a plastic bag and made my way through the fog of the university evening. I strolled through the austere, red-brick quadrangle and came to a building which looked as though it were ready to tumble into the court. Surely nobody lived in it?

The Professor did. He opened the door of his suite to me. He was not at all as I had imagined him. In my mind I saw a tall man with an imperious bald head and eyes that looked down his nose at the specks of dirt known as first year students. He was in fact a crumpled little man with thick black hair, startlingly alert eyes and the thinnest neck I have ever seen, like a bundle of stems disappearing into a vase.

"I'm Farrukh Dhondy," I said, forgetting the sentence I had prepared and had rehearsed again on the stairs.

"How very intersting," he said.

"I mean I've got something for you," I blurted, feeling foolish as soon as I'd said it.

"Promises," he said and he laughed to put me at my ease. "Stop fumbling at the doorstep, Farrukh Dhondy, and come in. You are expected."

"Expected?"

"Yes, expected. I warrant you are the son of the old Parsi collector R. S. Dhondy of Bombay fame. I have waited years. Do you drink sherry?"

"Grandson. Sometimes," I mumbled.

"You are his grandson sometimes?"

"No, sherry sometimes. He's dead. Long ago, twelve years back."

"What are you doing here?" he said and strolled across the oak-panelled room to a shelf with decanters and glasses.

"Natural Sciences," I said.

"Most unnatural, you should study classics. Alas, the old man, we knew each other well and he threatened me, grandson, he threatened me. You know what it is to believe and then to be shaken in that belief? Like Christopher Columbus actually coming across the waterfall at the end of the world?"

"No sir," I said.

"You come from Bombay? Splendid city. Always felt like a fly in treacle there. Spent many years . . ."

"I have . . ." I began.

"I know what you have, sir," he said as I hung on to the glass of sherry he handed me. "The document, yes? Don't tell me, it's in a locker at Waterloo station."

"No, sir, in this bag here."

"I might as well have it," he said. "Your grandfather spoke of it to me twenty years ago, but I have hung back. You are carrying a time bomb, young man."

"He left a note saying your name," I ventured.

He took the document from me looked hard at it and then dropped it on the carpet and paced to the window and back.

"Christopher Le Clerc. He existed. Your grandfather was on the right track."

"I am afraid I don't know anything, sir," I said.

"That is what I fear myself. Not you, but I. You know

young man, I have spent forty to fifty years studying the life of Christ. Lunatics and vain theoreticians come at me from every angle. Your grandad was different. Tell me, was he religious?"

"I didn't know him well, sir, he died before I was old enough to think about him."

"I have wasted my life nosing around," he said. "To your grandfather this manuscript was curious, perhaps frightening. To me, it might be a tight little noose." He put his fingers around his neck and squeezed. "But I suppose I'd better look at it."

He reached for the document, lit a lamp in the corner and undid the seal. I could see he was breathing with a pace of excitement.

"Are you a Christian?" he asked and then laughed. "Don't answer me. Leave me with the time bomb."

"You want I should go?"

"Not in the least. I beg you to stay. I am going to tell you an incredible story. One that will stir the world."

The professor sat me down. He refilled my glass. He told me this:

"Your grandfather, God rest his soul, has sent me from beyond the grave the deposition, the story, of one Christopher Le Clerc. This chappy was a monk, a missionary. He went out with the East India Company to Bengal in the eighteenth century. There he found Christ."

"I thought you said he was already . . ."

"No, I mean found him, actually found him."

"How . . ."

"Hush. This is your grandfather's story. He, Le Clerc, I mean, was a man of high family and calling. In India, two hundred years ago, he heard of a legend of a stone in a hillside with a carving of a pair of hands with blood dripping from wounds in the palms, palms pierced with nails, you know the sort of thing. Curious, but not unusual.

He was taken by the legend and claims that he went with an Indian government survey expedition into the Himalayas to research the legend. There are records of that expedition in the archives. I've looked that up in the India Office. The expedition, seven men, disappeared, they think in a blizzard. That was 1791.

Ten years later, a man appears in a Hindu religious monastery in the north of India. Nowadays, there's hippies and religious middle class kids and all sorts hanging around India, but in those days it was extremely unusual, for a white man to turn Hindu and go around with bare feet and his head shaved, begging alms in the market places. The British authorities were disturbed. They thought he was an army deserter and they arrested him and took him in leg irons to England. This man claimed to be Christopher Le Clerc. He didn't want to co-operate with the authorities. He told them only that he had been with the expedition, had been lost in a blizzard that lasted several days, had his life saved by some natives, and had ended up by living eight years amongst a tribe of people unknown to civilisation who claimed to be Christians.

"So far so good. Nothing unusual in that. But this man claimed that he had discovered in India the tomb of Jesus Christ himself. The tribe he claimed to have lived with had been visited, some seventeen to eighteen hundred years before, by a man who claimed to be Jesus Christ. That was his sensation. Do you see dear boy? Your grandfather then gets this document from the monastery. It tells the whole story. At least I hope it does. Christ didn't die upon the cross. He spent his last days in some mountain fastness in India. God help us."

The professor's voice trailed away.

"What happened to Le Clerc?"

"Unimportant," the Professor said, pacing back to the window. Then he made a strange clucking sound with his tongue. I remember that most clearly, it comes back to me in my sleep to this day. "We don't believe him, dear boy, but your grandfather did. Do you see why I approach this . . . this thing with the greatest caution? From what I have found out these last years, Le Clerc was locked away as a madman, then as an impostor, and then released. Tolerated and set free. Frightening."

"Why frightening?"

"Because Le Clerc, this Indian monk claiming to be him, may have been a fake or he may have brought to civilisation the most startling revelation that the so called Christian world has known. What your grandfather said to me, the old heathen, was that this brown folder contains the gospel of Jesus Christ himself. A fifth gospel. Not by the disciples Matthew, Luke, Mark and John but by our saviour himself. It's a dreadful moment, dear boy, a dreadful moment for me. I am a Christian you see. The secret destroyed Le Clerc. All these years I have kept away from it for it might destroy me."

These things I did not understand. It was a fascinating story but not the kind to sweat over.

"I'm going to read it tonight. What time is breakfast at your college?"

I told him and he asked me to be back at eight-thirty the next morning.

I did as he asked. The cleaners were on the stairs and one of them turned to me and said that Professor Jardin was not to be disturbed.

"Sleeps on Mondays, he does."

The professor must have heard her, because he came out on the landing in his scarlet dressing gown and ushered me into his rooms.

He looked twenty years younger than he had the previous night, or maybe it was the morning sun picking out the wrinkles on his face and throwing clean shadows on his skin that gave it a freshness. The waxen smoothness of the night before had reminded me of impending death.

He was solemn and brushed his long hair back.

"Sit down. I've opened it and read it. The fifth gospel is obviously authentic. It's in Latin. Do you have any Latin?"

"No," I confessed.

"Now this stays with me and you. It's in a sense your property. I'm going to read some of it to you."

"I'd be grateful, sir," I said.

"Le Clerc has left a map of the Kingdom of Issavali, the lost Christian tribe. I've checked it's co-ordinates in the survey of India and it's the uncharted part of the Himalayas. Shall I translate for you. A monk writing not to mother church, but for the Hindus of his monastery."

This is, briefly, what I remember of what he said:

"This tribe of Issavali found Le Clerc in the snows. His expedition companions were dead. They found him with a cross around his neck and they revived him and restored him. He lived with them eight years. He tells the story of the tribe, a civilisation that had lived isolated, hundreds of years. He describes the valley and then tells the story of the coming of Christ to that valley. What is important is what the gospel says. The fifth gospel. It is a history written by Christ himself. He arrives in Issavali after surviving crucifixion, after wandering in Iran and Asia Minor and begging a living for years. It's all there, just as it is in the other gospels, the story of John the Baptist, of Mary and Joseph, of his birth and his miracles and his assembling of disciples. That's where it gets curious. In the fifth gospel, there are only eleven disciples. Simon called Peter, Matthew, Luke, John, Thomas, Jacob, James the Son of Alphaeus, Philip, Bartholomew, Simon called Zelotes, Jude the brother of James. There is no mention of Judas Iscariot. And in the story of the crucifixion, there is no betrayal, no thirty pieces of silver, no kiss in the garden, nothing.

"Naturally he asked them what became of the saviour. They took him to the tomb. On the tomb were still carved the words 'Noli Me Tangere', which means 'Do not touch me'. Le Clerc saw the body, preserved through the ages by cold and care, of Jesus Christ, god bless us."

It was then that the professor asked me for a promise. I was not to say what I had heard from him. I left him to get to lunch at college. Two days later the detectives called at my digs. For me it was the end of that episode. I had done what my mother had asked me to do, what my grandfather had willed before he died.

For years the mystery of the disappearance of James Jardin haunted the minds of people who had known him. The word got around that I had told the police that I had delivered an important document to him the day before he disappeared. I carried on with my studies and put the professor out of my mind. Two years after that a television company came to me and asked if I would help them with a documentary film they were making about the mystery surrounding the professor's disappearance. I had made him a promise and I turned down the invitation. The programme was made anyway and I watched it. It traced professor Jardin's life and talked a bit about some discoveries he had made about the life of Christ through his readings of documents. Small things which made me smile. I left Cambridge and England forever when I finished my degree and went back to India. After five years I forgot the professor. Then a friend of mine in Bombay asked me to go on a trip with him to a remote ashram, a monastery of Hindu monks who practiced meditation and lived away from the India I knew. I went.

That was where I discovered Jardin again. Shaved head, bare feet, the begging bowl and the strange clucking sound of the tongue, a white monk amongst the rest, a boil on a brown face.

"Professor Jardin," I said.

"Dead," he said.

"Unmistakeable. You remember me?"

The monk in saffron smiled.

"Tell me, is this the monastery to which Le Clerc came?"

The monk nodded.

"Will you speak to me? I kept your secret. My grand-father's wish that only you should know."

"That you did. Come with me," he said, "but no talk of Jardin. I am Gurusatva, the priest, the disciple of Vishnu, the creator . . ."

"Yes, I understand," I interrupted.

It was later that afternoon that he told me the rest of his story. It had been ten years. He was still learning the vocation of being a Hindu monk. He was anxious that his life in Britain, now that he was an old man and probably at the end of his years, should not touch his belief. He had been happy to have disappeared.

"The file is still open," I said to him.

"Closed," and he shut his eyes.

"Tell me."

"Dear boy," he said. "You brought me that document and I fled with it. What I know now belongs to you. I want no part of it. I shall never say it again, so take it away with you. Le Clerc was right about almost everything. His map was an excellent guide. I left Cambridge that night after stealing a passport from an American tourist whom I sat next to in Great St Mary's Church. I was disturbed by what I had read, I was Christian, remember. I went to church for guidance and there it struck me. I had to know for myself. I had spent years with papers, now I wanted evidence in the flesh. I stole the passport by giving the tourist some bullshit about being a professor. No doubt the police caught up with him and my misdemeanor. I came to India and took a train to the township Le Clerc mentions. It took me forty days of trekking to find the stone carving that Le Clerc refers to. There was dynamite in my pack. I dismissed my bearers and camped there for two days and then I blasted the rock. Sure enough there was a chasm in the mountain.

It was a passageway of ice and it took me three days to get to the valley beyond. That valley exists and the Christians exist."

The professor clucked his tongue.

"They received me. Le Clerc had told them, it seems, that others would follow him into the valley, a prophecy that they passed down.

"It was four years that I lived with them and learnt their language. They have a group of eleven elders who speak a very rough kind of Hebrew, the language of the man they think was Christ. I told them stories from the bible. I won their confidence and after those years they took me up to the tomb of Christ. I saw with my own eyes the body of the man preserved in the eternal snows, the man who had called himself Jesus Christ of Nazareth. The body is clearly, with its garments welded to it by cold and time, the body of a once handsome Jew. I asked to examine the body. Its arms were folded across the chest. The one question that kept nagging me was why? why had the Nazarene abandoned his disciples and come to this god forsaken place?

"Then the revelation. There are no marks on the body. The hands bear no sign of crucifixion. The elders kept the text of the fifth gospel. When we got back to the valley I asked to see the original copy. It was as Le Clerc had transcribed it. It was then I told them of the twelfth disciple, of Judas Iscariot who had betrayed Jesus. Eleven, they said, only eleven. I repeated, perhaps foolishly, my story—Judas was a twelfth disciple, he betrayed Jesus, that's how Jesus came to die and be resurrected.

"Who was this Judas I spoke of? they asked. How could a man betray the Christ and live with himself? I knew the answer. And you know the answer dear boy."

"I think I do," I said.

"Then they asked me why their saviour had not written this down if I had brought knowledge of it from the outside world. I didn't know what to answer. Perhaps he roamed the world, this Judas, I said, and came to a valley where he spread the word of Jesus Christ. The traitor became the betrayed. It was the greatest act of repentance that Jesus himself preached. The man you have there in the tomb . . .

"They put me in a prison hut. Day and night I heard the eleven elders arguing. Now and then they would send in a messenger to ask me a question about the gospels I knew from the outer world. On the eighth day of my imprisonment the wrath of nature visited the valley. I heard the rumbling as I lay on my mat. A rumble like an earthquake, like tanks running through crowded streets my boy.

"My jailer said, 'You have brought this evil into the valley of Christ.'

"The avalanches descended on the valley. The people fled their homes. They went up the mountain slopes. I was left alone in the confusion and walked out free into the sapphire dark of that night. I ran. A vast barrage of white fell into the valley, throwing back the light of the moon. Do you want to know how I got away?"

"No," I said, "I want to know why you are here. Why are you a Hindu, why did you choose to disappear? The police came to me, in England, I mean."

"I am sorry, dear boy," he said. "You kept your silence but I didn't keep my faith. Jai Vishnu. You can see I've put Christianity and all that behind me."

"Is that all?" I asked Jardin. "Who shall I tell?"

"Tell nobody. Or tell everybody," he said. "I no longer care and I'm sure Judas won't mind."

Lost Soul

Lost Soul

I suppose I should have, but I didn't see the transformation coming. The first I heard of it was when Mr Patel, Nakul's father, brought me his written list of complaints early one morning. What was to be done with the boy?

"You didn't have to write it down," I said. "He'll think you're filing it for the police."

"Devil is inside the boy," Mr Patel said, sadly, not ferociously.

"The devil isn't bothered if you file his sins," I said.

Mr Patel shook his head to say that he agreed.

"This is for the pundit. Hindu priest. Exact information."

"So you're convinced it's the devil," I said.

"Convinced hundred per cent," replied Mr Patel.

How could I contradict him? There was, at least for him, no other explanation. The list was long and weird. Nakul had been such a good boy. The change had turned him butterfly to caterpillar.

I first met him three years before the day he went . . . well, let us say three years before I filled in the form which said "Nakul Patel is at grave risk". I had moved in to a flat three doors down from the H.N. Stores, a grocery owned by Patel senior above which his family lived. Nakul soon made friends with me. I could feel him conquering a staggering shyness to ask me if he could pat my dog, give it a bone from the shop's freezer. Later he used to walk the dog and lounge around my flat and do small errands for me. He used to ask me about social work, what I did, why I wanted to help Asians and so on. Now his dad was approaching me for professional advice.

"National health is sometimes hiring psychiatrist," Mr Patel said. "How much these thing costs?"

"You won't have to pay a penny," I said.

"Not for psychiatrist, but what about a guru, they won't pay it one?"

"I'm afraid not," I said. "Does your guru cost money?"

"Lots money. Maybe three, five, eight hundred pound."

"Mr Patel, that's ridiculous!"

"For chasing devil?"

"For anything. But look, Patel Sahib," I said. (I often called him that and he accepted it.) In the S.S. we have a provision under section one for anything the child needs if it is at risk."

"Gambling?" Mr Patel asked. "Taking risk?"

"No, 'at risk'. It means if he's likely to get into trouble."

"Get *into*? He can't get out!"

He thrust the list at me again.

I glanced at accusation number 1. It said "Calling mother name."

"What's that?"

"Calling always."

"What, by her Christian name?"

"She is Hindu."

"I mean her first name? Does he get rude and call her by her first name?"

"She have one name and he call it, instead of saying 'mummy'."

"And this second thing here? What do you mean 'don't sit till'? Sit still?"

"No, till. In shop. Nakul don't sit till."

"They don't look too serious to me, Patel Sahib. Those complaints. It'll pass."

"Read on," he said and crossed his hands behind his back waiting for some sympathy to tear itself away from me once the truth hit home.

3. Saying "bloody" and several dirty.

4. Calling all Gujerati uncles and mens "John".

5. Phoning up wrong numbers and shouting "This is meals on wheels, your goose is cooked."

6. Taking three saris from uncle's cloth shop and distributing free of charge to slag Asian girls outside Hindi cinema which his aunt herself saw.

7. Mixing price labels in grocery. Make some English persons, customer, very disturbed.

8. It all start when Nakul cut his hair like skinhead. He takes fifteen pounds from his mother for hire of Indian musical instrument and buy Dr Martin shoe.

The first part of number eight stunned me. "Nakul? Scalped?"

"True."

9. Three day ago he is gone completely under power of this crazy. He gone with one other Asian boy and throw himself in the police station shouting he is illegal immigrant. Police bring him back and tell me they waste sixteen hours of their time checking to find it is lies.

10. Go to our family doctor, Dr Hussein, and say he is having sickness in morning and his chest is growing and all things like he is going to have baby. Dr Hussein ring me up and tell me to help him to see psychiatrist. I told him he is doing it for nonsense and nuisance.

11. Take telephone out of the house on to street and give it to all passers-by. He is telling me they have to getting their calls.

12. Making experiments in arrangement design with pages of Hindu holy book.

13. Drinking vodka, Ribena mixture. Ribena is 98p a bottle.

14. Mowing lawn with Hoover.

15. Sticking needles and pins in little sister's dolls for put curse on outside persons, like teacher and police.

16. Not went to mathematics exam last week, I just find out. Letter come from his headmaster. He can't go in six form like this.

17. Spoil all groceries by painting Hitler moustache on all faces, even baby faces on nappy packet. Have to put special offer with moustache.

18. Got uncle attached to toilet seat with special glue.

19. Yesterday I catch him gone to sleep when he was supposed to go in the evening to special accountancy class paid for by his uncle. When I asked him why he is asleep he keep eyes closed and answer in gruff voice. He say the ghost of some white singer is come into him.

20. Nearly worst thing: he bring two dog he is find on the pavement and bring them into the shop door to do dirty sex things and start laughing when the lady customer come. I beat all three.

21. Too bad.

"So you left it out?" I asked.

"To a Hindu I can talk it. He must understand."

"You can't tell me? I'm very curious," I said.

"It is all to do with left hand and right hand, sir. British don't know these things."

I suppose I was content not to know. I got the drift of the other twenty anyway.

"Where is the lad now?" I asked.

"Locked up in a dark room. He went to sleep."

"It seems to me all perfectly natural if a bit too lively," I said. "Come on, Mr Patel, it's Britain. He's bored with life, a bit fed up with his uncles' and family's advice. Wild oats, it's not serious."

"He speak in different languages."

"Languages?"

"Every languages."

"Can I come and see him?" I asked.

"I have consult all my relatives, they are coming," Mr Patel said.

"About what?"

"Beating Nakul and these things."

"You're not beating him, surely. He's almost a grown man, for Christ's sake."

"He feel nothing. Only the demon inside feel and shout in different voices."

"Voices."

"Yes," said Mr Patel, "like Kate Bush and sometime American accent."

I promised I would go as soon as I was dressed. It sounded serious enough. I used to visit their house and had been specifically invited on two or three occasions for religious ceremonies. It was Nakul who had explained the ceremonies to me. One for new year, one for harvest. Nakul told me the stories of the proceedings without conviction, passing on something he had learnt. And now, according to Mr Patel, there had to be an exorcism.

Nakul's mother answered the door. She had her sari over her head and she'd been crying. She didn't speak much English. She ushered me into the front room at the top of the stairs. The men were having a conference.

There were about six of them including Mr Patel. As always, tea was brought by Nakul's sister. In the background there was a scream. Some of the uncles cocked an ear to it, trying to pick up in the sound the precise characteristics of the demon. Then Nakul's voice broke through and a song followed. It did sound weird. Not like a boy singing in the bath.

"See it worst," Mr Patel said.

"It is noisy," I said.

The fat Mr Patel spoke, Nakul's father's distant cousin, the one with the daughter whom the family hoped would marry Nakul when he finished sixth form and accountancy. The fat Mr Patel was from Uganda. Nakul's father was from Kenya. Their grandfathers had shared the same village in Gujerat; they hoped their children would share the same freehold roof in Tooting.

The fat Mr Patel knew about these things. For the past two hours he had been with Nakul. He knew the symptoms. It was a demon all right. He spoke fast in Gujerati. Then they translated for me. The fat Mr Patel had measured Nakul's arms and his waist. It was necessary. He had heard the demon speak and had held a conversation with the demon while Nakul, poor boy, lay unconscious.

"You interveiwed the demon?" I asked.

"I was trying to find who is his special enemy," the fat Mr Patel said.

Apparently that was the procedure. The demon himself would name whom he most feared. Then you hired that person to chase the demon away. Logic. The fat Mr Patel brandished some branches of a neem tree which had been imported and sold to them for the special purpose of sweeping demons.

"It shouted something chronically," Mr Patel said.

"Did you discover its enemies?"

"It gave me a phone number."

"Phone number?"

The fat Mr Patel produced a slip of paper on which he had written the number he had managed to wheedle out of the demon. The conference decided to call the number. They dialled it and we waited.

A secretary answered. It was the ashram of a Dr Ananda Vidhya Bharati, Hindu pundit, Sanskrit scholar, scourge of all demons this side of the Ganges.

94

The good Dr couldn't speak to them just then. He was in meditation, but yes, he did undertake such work. The conference would wait till the doctor came out of his meditation.

The theory was floated that this particular demon that had possessed Nakul was obviously white. The white world had a lot of free souls floating about. The wickedness of the white world was such that some souls couldn't even find new bodies to inhabit. They had to turn spiritual pirate. This was obviously what had happened to poor Nakul and changed him from a nice flared-trousered, long-haired, obedient boy to a swearing skinhead.

I told Mr Patel that I wanted to be kept in touch, but that I had to go at that point.

When I came back that afternoon the uncles were still there. The good Dr Bharati had been consulted. He couldn't do a thing for less than a thousand pounds. They could go elsehwere if they wanted, but he was not a man to trifle with. He specialised in white demons. He'd lived in Canada and the U.S.A.

"He will take only one pound for himself," Mr Patel said. He looked impressed and gloomy. "The rest is for modern equipment."

"Equipment?"

"White demons don't understand Sanskrit prayers and Hindu ceremonies. They have to scare with modern equipments."

"We are in some agreement," Mr Patel said. Some of the uncles, according to their seniority in the family and their wealth had promised certain sums. What could he do? He was not such a rich man. Thank God he had understanding relatives. Even so, some money was short. It wasn't a big sum.

"This is first member of this generation to be catch by devil," Mr Patel said and as he spoke there was another piercing scream from Nakul upstairs followed by a low gurgling melody that withdrew abruptly when we strained to listen.

The Patels embraced each other over the agreement. Hope was in the air again. The good Dr would restore the boy to normality and revive the family's reputation. I felt that secretly Mr Patel was somewhat proud of playing host to a demon, a British demon at that.

I wanted to say, even at this stage, even after committing section one money from the social services, that I didn't believe in demons.

"My grandfather, someone put spell on him in our village," the fat Mr Patel said. "That is worst when somebody does to you because they are jealous."

"How does one do it?"

"Many different ways. In my grandfather case, they tied a string to a fish's neck and let it loose in the sea. When fish is in calm water then my grandfather heart is calm, when it is in troubled current, my grandfather also troubled and shaking like a fish." He indicated how with his hands.

"Fish don't have necks," I objected.

They looked at me as though I was raising irrelevant points. I felt a bit contrite. It wasn't the right thing to have said.

"And there'll be some money from section one, of course," I said.

"How much?" the fat Mr Patel asked.

"Substantial amounts," I replied.

Now squeezing money from section one is not like getting blood from a stone, more like juice from a rather dried up orange. It's there but there's never enough of it.

Two days after the conference I saw to it that Her Majesty's Department of Health and Social Security had made a contribution to the expulsion of a particularly nasty and multi-cultural demon in Balham. I went to see how the exorcism would go. It had occurred to me that perhaps Nakul had gone stark staring bonkers, but I dared not mention it to the assembled uncles. It would be seen as more obstruction. Besides demons were welcome, relatively speaking. They were familiar. Madness was not.

The house was crammed by the time Dr Ananda Vidhya Bharati stepped out of a mini-cab. Relatives, well-wishers and friends had come to witness the battle. I was astonsihed when I set eyes on Dr Bharati. He looked very young. He had a shaved head with a little fountain of hair emerging in an inky squirt from the back. He wore a brown raw-silk drape which covered everything from shins to breast. It was wrapped in a failing diagonal across him and he wore slippers, what they call Jesus-creepers. He had chalk marks on his head to emphasise his holiness and he wore dark glasses. Marvellous touch.

I think the Patels were also taken aback by his youth. A white girl, disciple or secretary, fussed over him, carrying a brief case and a couple of silver trays. The good Dr was garlanded. It was too late to start objecting about his youth. He couldn't have been a day older than twenty-five and possibly he was much younger.

He said he would start work straight away. He blessed the threshold and the waiting crowd was impressed. Children peeped from the top of the stairs and from round the counters of the grocery store which remained open for business. The younger toddlers clutched their mothers' saris.

The good Dr wanted to see Nakul straight away. He would invoke the power of the old Hindu gods of course, but they might fail to impress this stray white soul. He might have to use modern equipment. He had ordered it. The cardboard cartons should be sent straight up to him. They could be left in the corridor outside the patient's room. Was that possible?

All things were possible, Mr Patel said. This fellow looked a really humble exorcist.

The reports were not good. The demon had been playing up the previous day. It had demanded to eat beef and pork and other forbidden stuff. Horrible. The exorcist went up to the chamber. We waited in the front room. There were screams from upstairs, and shouts. The fat Mr Patel nodded. All this was familiar. It was the first stage. How funny, only the week before he had been describing the scene to Nakul, how the brahmin in his village had actually had to wrestle with the victim of a demon and how they had set fire to another one by burning the victim at the stake. Nothing happened to the victim, only the demon felt the flames and screamed till it couldn't take it any more.

Was Dr Bharati winning?

The front doorbell rang and a delivery van unloaded several large cardboard boxes in the name of Dr Bharati. They were paid for by Mr Patel and sent upstairs forthwith.

In an hour's time a new sound wafted downstairs. It was the heavy thump of a bass guitar, the sound of drums through an amplified system. Dr Bharati appeared at the top of the stairs. He was exhausted. It was going well, but he was tired. It was like driving on the motorway, it was best to rest as even a split-second slip, a blink at the wrong moment, could be fatal.

It was all right. The demon was at rest too. In a few hours they would resume.

I didn't stay the night though several of the Patels did. The next morning Dr Bharati ordered breakfast and said he was eating with the demon, they had achieved a pact. Then, I was told, more screams were heard. Plates of sausages came floating out of the doorway and cups of coffee were thrown from the top of the stairs. The demon was reluctant to leave. By mid-morning the amplifiers had again been turned on and several sound and wah-wah machines were going. It sounded like a really bad disco, and above all the din there was the sound of Sanskrit prayer. Dr Bharati had settled down to a real three-pronged, multi-cultural attack.

And then the demon began to scream. It was horrible. It was not Nakul's voice and it wasn't Dr Bharati's gentle but firm and deep chanting bass. Then everything went silent. The Dr emerged. The demon was gone. Nakul was himself again. He was asleep. In leaving, the demon had held on to his rib-cage and shaken it as a prisoner does the bars of a jail. It was painful but Nakul was saved. Could the doctor have a word with Mr Patel and the other gentlemen?

They conferred. Tea was brought. Dr Ananda Vidhya Bharati was sure that Nakul would eventually be restored, but he had to take him away from his immediate home for the time being. Was that all right? Nakul should go and live with him in the ashram in north London. The Patel's looked at each other.

"You see," Dr Bharati said, "I find that Nakul is very weak on all his Gujerati and Indian culture. You haven't even taught him to meditate."

The Patels nodded. They explained. It was pretty impossible in Britain. They led such busy lives.

"That is why I will teach him. No extra charge. Only way," Dr Bharati said.

Again the Patels consulted. If the good Dr thought it was best. He wouldn't be able to go to the sixth form of course. He would have to suspend accountancy classes and no doubt the fat Mr Patel didn't want his daughter engaged to someone who was such fertile soil for demonic roots. Yes, Dr Bharati could take the boy away. He would visit them and show them his progress at the ashram.

Then the Dr went and fetched Nakul. He came down, dressed now in a kurta and white trousers. There was peace on his face. He touched his father's feet and humbly greeted and thanked his uncles. It was touching.

That day Nakul left with Dr Bharati. A couple of mini-cabs called for them. The equipment, which was now back in the cardboard boxes, was taken away too.

His mother shed a tear and his father and sisters hugged him. The son, the brother, the hope of the family had been restored.

It was six months after that restoration that I was working on another case. It was somewhat similar. It concerned a Gujerati boy who had turned skinhead and attacked some black people in a park. I spoke to him. He made very little sense to me. Something had snapped in his pattern of life. His father told me that he had been a good boy till he became suddenly possessed. I wasn't thinking of hiring an exorcist, but I thought that speaking to Nakul would help. He had been through it. I asked Mr Patel for the address of the ashram. He didn't have it. I traced it through the memory of the mini-cab driver from the firm down our road.

I went looking for Nakul one morning. I had to report on his progress too. And, anyway, Dr Ananda Vidhya Bharati and his powers or pretensions interested me. I was deposited by the mini-cab man in a street in Walthamstow. I walked up and down the street looking for Dr Bharati's ashram. Frankly, it wasn't the sort of place I'd expected. In my mind I had seen Dr Bharati in a mansion-like place with marble floors and carpets on which to meditate, supported financially and spiritually by hundreds of rich middle-class disciples.

Not so. There was no sign of an ashram. I went into the fish and chip shop and asked if there were any Indians on that street. Religious people.

"Don't know mate," I was told, "but there's freaks upstairs. Make a bloody racket I can tell you."

I stepped out. On the door to the upstairs there was a

sign. It said: NAK AND ANDY SOUND SYSTEM HIRE.

I rang the bell. There was the sound of boots on the stairs and "Andy" answered the door. He didn't recognise me, but I recognised him. His hair had grown.

"Yeah, what do you want mate?"

"Andy?" I asked.

"What about it?"

"I get it. And Nak is Nakul?"

"You want to hire a sound, mate?" the good Dr asked.

"No," I said. "An exorcist."

That hit him. He looked at me through squint eyes. He shouted up the stairs to Nakul.

Nak came charging down.

"Got a joker here," Andy said.

"That's no joker," Nakul said and called me up.

"This geezer's cool, relax," he said to Dr Ananda Vidhya Bharati. The room at the top of the stairs into which they invited me for a drink was jammed with electronic equipment.

On the speakers were painted the words LOST SOUL.

"Neat," I said.

Nakul didn't know why I had found him, he was a bit uncertain.

"You won't blow it, will you?"

"To your dad and the other Mr Patels?"

"Look, I had to do it," Nakul protested. "They wouldn't give me the money to do anything like this. We were bust and dad kept on about going back to school and marrying that fat arse and doing bloody accountancy. I had to get out."

"I see," I said.

"Give us a chance. In three months we'll have enough bread to hire clubs ourselves. Then we'll start rolling in it, mate. Plenty of Asian kids and black kids follow our sound.

It's new. Once I get hold of some loot, dad will forgive me anything. I can give them all their investment back."

"And the section one money?"

"That's on the house," Nakul said. "But, look, it worked didn't it?"

"How do you mean?"

"Well, they used to call me Nakul. I hated the name. Now they call me 'the Nak'."

He smiled. It was contagious.

Under Gemini

Under Gemini

In ancient India, in the days of the coming of Alexander the Great, there lived a wise and brave king called Porus. He had two sons born as twins under the star of Gemini. He called them Gav and Talkand. They looked identical, but two such different brothers you never saw. They grew to be splendid princes.

Gav was a thoughtful boy who would turn the skies grey from wondering why they were blue. Talkand was a young man with never a thought in the world but hunting and shooting and fighting and sport.

While Talkand rode out with falcon and sparrow hawk and spent his day in the wilds of the kingdom swimming mountain streams, daring himself to climb to snow peaks and ride for a hundred miles a day, teaching himself to be the best swordsman in Porus's kingdom, the best archer in Porus's armies, the tamer of elephants and a boxer and wrestler who could challenge the pluckiest and heaviest champions of the land, Gav stayed in the palace and read manuscripts. He played musical instruments and wrote new prayers to the gods.

From their birth, King Porus had entrusted the twins to the care of an old and trusted slave of his palace called Sassa. Sassa was a teacher to the lads. When he taught them to swim the rivers, Talkand would interest himself in striking out as fast as he could to the far shore. Gav would stand in the water and wonder why the current of the river flowed one way and not the other and what made the water foam. When Sassa instructed them in archery, Talkand attempted to bend the toughest bow and shoot the arrow to the limits of the horizon; Gav plucked at the strings of the bow and heard it's vibration, placed it against hollow tree trunks and made wondering play with the sounds. When Sassa took them on horseback to spear wild pigs, Talkand spurred his horse into the tusks of the cornered beast while Gav turned his eyes from the sight of blood.

Talkand brought the tusks of the beast back to his father.

"What did you bring, Gav?" King Porus asked.

Gav produced a picture he had drawn of his twin brother on horseback spearing the wild boar and you could see in the eyes of the beast, as the blood rushed out of it's pierced side, a haunted begging for mercy. The picture showed the horse from the side and the rider from his back.

"Why haven't you drawn your brother's features? The pride of the hunter at the moment of the kill?" King Porus asked.

"I can't draw my own face, flushed with pride at the sight of killing," Gav said. So much alike were they in the flesh.

When they were eighteen years old there came the invasion of Alexander the Greek. In the court of King Porus the messengers from the borders of the kingdom brought the news. The Greek army was encamped two hundred miles from the city.

"What does this Alexander want?" King Porus asked. "Doesn't he know that we are the mightiest power in the world?"

"He has overcome the kingdom of Nicaea, and he wants to be master of all India. He has promised this to his soldiers who are thirsty for the gold that they believe our land holds," the messengers said.

"We'll talk with him. We shall talk peace and prepare for

war," King Porus said. He sent for his sons. In the court there was a lot of trepidation. The stories had reached India of how Alexander's armies were unstoppable. They had swept across from Macedonia, across Persia and Afghanistan and were knocking at the gates, stalled at the passes of the mountains through which they threatened to pour down like lava on the kingdom of King Porus.

"We shall send out an ambassador to him," King Porus told the court in the presence of Gav and Talkand." We shall defy the Greek to set foot beyond the Khyber Pass. Yes, land we have, we shall tell him, plenty of land, enough for graves for all his Greek and Persian hordes."

Then Talkand spoke up. "Let me go and threaten him, father."

"You have other work to do, Talkand," the King said. "You are of age now and the best soldier in my whole army. I am getting old. I want you to start preparing for war. You shall be in charge of the army, the infantry, the elephant cavalry, the guns, the archers. You must begin within the hour to give instructions to the armourers, to appoint new officers and to pick the terrain for your battles with the Greeks."

Then the King turned to Gav. "And you will go to Alexander with an armed escort. You are a man of words. You will tell him that we Indians are not easy game, that King Porus will grant mercy to the boy Alexander and forgive him his fault of distracting our peace and our kingdom with his armies and rumours. Tell him he can turn back and go his way and we will not pursue him. We are generous."

"I have heard of this Alexander," Gav said. The court listened, hushed. "He is not a man to be trifled with. Half the known world has been conquered by him and we can talk of peace if we . . ."

"Peace?" King Porus demanded. "What peace, Gav? We

have the best army that India has known and the best general the world can provide in your brother Talkand. We shan't talk peace."

Gav was silent. The King instructed him and within two hours he was sent out with fifty-one soldiers to meet with Alexander's scouts and to deliver the message.

When he had gone, the King turned to Talkand.

"I have also heard that this Greek is a treacherous bastard. Your brother may never return alive. Alexander may hold him hostage."

"I would have gone," Talkand said.

"That was not my wish. You are going to prove that the undefeated Greeks have met their match. We sent him a royal prince to show him we are not afraid."

Talkand was puzzled. He was worried. He loved his twin brother, and he knew that if he issued their father's threat to Alexander, Gav would put himself in danger.

But Alexander didn't take Gav hostage. Gav returned in the space of six days. They were six days in which Talkand spent every hour instructing the armies and holding councils of war.

Gav rode back into the city, exhausted but at peace. He went straight away to report to King Porus.

"So Alexander has accepted? He will turn back?" the King asked.

"No," Gav replied.

"Did you give him my message?"

"No, father, I did not. I rode into his camp. He received me courteously. He asked me to rest after the long journey and showed me great hospitality. I spent some hours looking around his camp. He has a host of archers, Persian archers and Macedonian marksmen. He has battalions of cavalry and . . ."

"I don't want to know what toys Alexander plays with," the King said. "Tell me what you said."

"I saw the strength of his armies and I feared for our kingdom," Gav replied. "The Greeks are well prepared. I offered them a treaty."

"A treaty? I didn't ask you to offer a treaty." The king was furious. Talkand interrupted him.

"Let us hear what my brother has to say."

Gav continued. "I told him that war would mean bloodshed, but we could settle the war by agreeing to give him, Alexander, all the land on the other side of the Indus river if he promised on his honour to respect our kingdom beyond it . . ."

"Traitor!" The King was on his feet. "Talkand. Put this traitor under arrest. Take him away, the coward. I don't want to set eyes on him."

Then the king turned to Sassa.

"Is this how you have educated my son? To turn against me and my wishes when we are threatened with conquest?"

Gav said nothing. He looked around the court. Then Talkand stepped forward and touched his twin brother on the shoulder.

"If I am the general of the armies, I shall take charge of him," he said and he led Gav away. Sassa followed them.

"Why don't you repent and apologise to your father. If it's war, you can join your brother."

Gav didn't reply.

"Sassa, you look after him," Talkand said to the old slave. "My father will never forgive him until we have won the war. Then I shall speak to him myself. I know my brother. He will never repent."

Talkand left Gav in a far sanctuary of the palace with only Sassa to attend to him and went about the business of preparing for Alexander.

That night Gav sent Sassa to fetch his brother.

When Talkand came, Gav said, "I know the numbers and

strengths of Alexander's troops. We must match them.''

While Talkand listened carefully, Gav told him about the opposing army's squadrons of cavalry, lines of foot soldiers, elephant brigades, archers and about their lines of command.

"What else did you learn while you were at their camp?" Talkand asked. "That Alexander is their supreme commander, their great Champion. Without him they would not have conquered half the world. If you can kill or capture their commander, you have won the war."

It was in the thick of the rainy season that news reached Talkand that Alexander's armies had crossed the Khyber and camped on the other side of the River Indus. The Greeks had marched in the night under cover of darkness. They had made the first move. Parties of their foot soldiers had crossed the river and two battalions of Greeks had set up a V-shaped formation beyond it, with bridges built behind them to the main body of their army.

Sassa brought the news to Gav.

"And what has my brother done?"

"He has sent the cavalry after them to break their lines in the centre."

"Is Talkand in the palace?"

"In the palace? He is leading them himself."

"And my father?"

"Talkand has kept King Porus away from the battlefield. The King wouldn't listen to him at first, but Talkand has persuaded him."

"Does Alexander lead his own men?"

"You seem very interested in this battle. Why don't you beg the King to let you go and fight by your brother's side?" Sassa asked.

"I want to help Talkand. But you know I am no good with a sword or a spear. I can help him from here."

"From here?"

"Yes. What my brother needs is not a feeble soldier by his side, but a plan of action."

"Maybe. But until you beg your father, you won't even get a glimpse of the battlefield. You are under arrest, remember?" Sassa objected.

"You can be my eyes and ears. Sassa, bring me some sticks of wood and a carving knife."

Sassa thought the cowardly prince had lost his mind but he did as he was told.

The next day he brought him news of the battle again. As he walked into the room he saw Gav squatting on the floor. He had drawn out a field in chalk and on it he had placed several little carved figures.

"Bad news," Sassa said.

"What's happened on the battlefield? Did the formation of Greek infantry give way?"

"Talkand made a mistake," Sassa reported. "He sent out the cavalry to attack the forward foot soldiers of the Greeks, but Alexander had forded the river in two more places and it looked for an hour or two as though we were going to smash their centre. But no sooner had our cavalry broken through their lines than other foot soldiers replaced them. Our horse retreated."

"Retreated? Weren't they supported by our own foot soldiers?" Gav asked. He was now pacing the floor.

"No, Prince, they were forced to retreat. They suffered heavy casualties."

"Doesn't Talkand realise that only foot soldiers can hold ground? He can use cavalry as raiders, but not to hold territory. Is my brother safe?"

"Yes, he's safe. Slightly wounded, but back at camp."

"Can you fetch him to me Sassa?"

"He is very busy. He keeps a council with our officers tonight."

"Tell him he must come. Tell him that this battle must be

fought under the star of Gemini. We are twins, we are one."

Sassa took the message to Talkand, but Talkand did not come.

Again at the end of the third and fourth day, Sassa brought news of the battle to Gav. He had observed it from the turrets of the city wall and he didn't have happy news.

"The Greek cavalry has forded the river and stands supported by the foot soldiers. They are immoveable. Slowly this cunning Greek gains ground."

"What else?" Gav asked, and Sassa saw him return to the toys he had made on the floor and shift his pieces of carved wood.

"The Greek elephant squadrons have moved to the bridge behind the foot soldiers. It is expected that they will cross the river tomorrow. Our own elephant troops are to pass through our infantry tonight."

"And what news of Alexander himself?"

"He has been seen. Prince Talkand spotted him at the head of the cavalry and rushed with a troop of archers towards him, but he held ground behind his own personal guard of foot."

Again Gav moved his pieces of carving.

"You fool around with your carving while our Kingdom is in danger," Sassa protested.

"Fetch Talkand for me. I can see what the Greek is up to," Gav said, looking up from his little field on the floor.

"He will not come, Prince," Sassa replied.

"All right, then," Gav said. "Take him this prediction. Tell him I made it. Tomorrow the Greek cavalry and archers will move over open ground to their left, towards the city walls. From behind them will come supporting infantry. Alexander will not attack the lines we have drawn up to the right, in front of his bridges."

It was at the end of the evening of the next day that Sassa came back to Gav.

"It was as you said," he pronounced. "What magic have you . . ."

"Not magic," Gav said. "Logic. So far he has managed to trip Talkand's advance. Now he is setting a trap."

As Gav was saying this to Sassa, Talkand walked into the chamber.

"Sassa gave me your message and your prediction," he said. He looked tired. Talkand glanced at the little carvings on the floor.

"Don't venture out at the head of your troops tomorrow, brother," Gav said.

"I think we have the Greeks on the run. They pulled back two companies of archers on the right front today," Talkand said.

"Your place tomorrow is by King Porus. Stay in the city walls and throw your foot soldiers forward so that the elephant squadron can move to outside the city," Gav said.

Talkand looked impatient and exasperated.

"Come here," Gav called to him and led him to the floor where the carved pieces stood as he had arranged them.

"Look, this is Alexander. This is our side, our foot soldier battalions. I have placed them as accurately as I can according to Sassa's reports." Gav touched a carved piece and moved it forward on the field he had drawn. "You must give our elephant cavalry a chance to get across the field fast. At present they hold all the territory in front of them, but they must move to the side. They are obstructed by one squad of foot soldiers."

"You've gone crazy," Talkand said. "If I order those soldiers to advance, they'll be slaughtered."

"That's the price you have to pay," Gav said.

"Seven hundred men? Why can't they retreat?"

"They have to hold ground further up, right to the banks of the river. There's no time to bother about them, Talkand. Leave them there. The cavalry is required outside the

113

city. The Greeks have moved their whole attack towards it."

"You play your games, leave the war to me," Talkand said.

The brothers looked at each other. Then Talkand left.

It was the afternoon of the next day when Sassa burst into the chamber where Gav was held.

His face told the story. In the near distance, Gav could hear the clash of swords and the screams of men, the panic in the streets and the sounds of death.

"They are upon us. The Greeks."

"Where's Talkand?"

"He didn't take your advice. He rode out at the head of his troops this morning. It was as you said. Alexander led the assault on the city himself. We've lost."

"The Greeks chose their own battleground," Gav said. "What of my father?"

"He fought like a madman. When he heard of the state of the battle, he put on his armour and rushed out. Alexander gave instructions to surround him but not to kill him. There's no retreat. Their forces are inside the city and have surrounded the palace."

Gav sat down on the floor. He moved a few of the carved pieces. He stared at them, stunned.

The news of Talkand's death was brought to King Porus in the palace by Alexander himself.

"Do what you will with me, Greek," King Porus said.

"You have fought bravely and given your son in this battle," Alexander the conqueror said. "I have never met a foe as brave as this young man and if I could turn back the clock, I would he were alive. You've lost your son, but not your dignity and not your kingdom. Though it has cost me more blood than any other campaign, I give you your kingdom back. When this young man first came to negotiate with me, he talked of peace. He talked of a treaty. He seemed to me a coward. How wrong I was. I have witnessed him these last six days of our war fighting like a demon. I will leave you to your sorrow, King Porus. It is not easy to lose an only son."

King Porus's eyes were clouded with tears.

"My only son," he said as Alexander bowed his head and walked backwards out of his presence.

Then King Porus lifted the body of Talkand in his frail old arms and carried him through the corridors of the palace to Gav's chamber.

"You look like him, and that's strange," King Porus said to Gav. "He fought today as a man has never fought. The Greek mistook you for him. He thought today that my only son had died and I did not correct him. He was my only son. You sat here, playing with your stupid toys while he gave his life."

King Porus stepped forward and kicked the little carved pieces that Gav had placed on the floor.

"I turn my back on you," he said to Gav. "When they talk of our kingdom in times to come, they will remember Talkand, the warrior, the bravest man Alexander had the honour to fight. And you, you did nothing. You will be remembered for nothing."

And so saying, the old king, filled with fury and sorrow, spat in the face of his living son and turned his back for ever on the man who will be remembered, when all the defeated heroes are forgotten, as the inventor of chess.